ANNABELLE SAMI   ILLUSTRATED BY DANIELA SOSA

Agent Zaiba
INVESTIGATES

THE MISSING DIAMONDS

LiTTLE TiGER
LONDON

1
MEHNDI MADNESS

"Detective's log number thirty five. The time is..." Zaiba glanced at her watch. "15:00 hours. Location: The Royal Star Hotel, Farnworth, the United Kingdom. Observation and hiding point secured. This is Agent Zaiba."

Zaiba shuffled further back beneath an empty dining table, clutching her favourite book of all time, *Eden Lockett's Detective Handbook*. Eden Lockett might be made up, but her books were based on real crimes and she could teach a budding detective anything they needed to know about sleuthing. In her mysteries, she'd battled robbers and escaped tigers, a ghost in a mansion and villains in a circus. Zaiba flicked through the pages.

There! Advice about blending in with your surroundings: *Avoid bright colours. Now is not the time to make a fashion statement.*

Zaiba glanced down at her outfit. She was wearing a shiny blue shalwar kameez with a silver dupatta tossed over one shoulder. Hmmm. The perfect outfit for a pre-wedding Mehndi party sure, but when trying to hide from her arch nemesis? Not so good.

Although perhaps arch nemesis was a *bit* too harsh. Zaiba's cousin, Mariam, was on the other side of the room sandwiched between her parents. At least she had been on Zaiba's last sweep of the room. Things had been tense between them ever since Mariam decided to be born on the exact same day as Zaiba. Well, one year later. But couldn't she have waited a day or two at least? The latest incident in the growing feud had been at their annual joint birthday party last week. Mariam had accused Zaiba of hitting the unicorn piñata too hard. Seriously – how could anyone hit a piñata *too* hard? Zaiba could practically feel Mariam's icy stare piercing through the tablecloth, sending a shiver down her spine.

She turned the page in *Eden Lockett's Detective Handbook* to read one of many notes scribbled in the margin. She traced a finger round the familiar loops and curls. This and the mystery stories had been her mum's and she'd made lots of comments across her beloved book collection. Now they belonged to Zaiba, who had spent hours searching for each unique scribbling. It was her special way of getting to know her mum, who she called Ammi.

This message was a particular favourite of hers:

Better put on my brave pants today!

Zaiba smiled to herself. Her ammi had been funny. At least, she *thought* she had been funny. She'd passed away when Zaiba was too young to remember. Whenever Zaiba tried to ask her dad about what happened, he would repeat the same phrase, "Leave the past in the past." She always had the feeling that there was something her dad wasn't telling her. Something left to uncover...

Zaiba refocused her mind and peered out from beneath the tablecloth. Beyond the dining table the party was getting busier. Even though the event had officially started quite a while ago, three o'clock was still considered early for a party that would go on into the early hours of the morning. The guests that had just arrived, wearing jewel-coloured saris and sharply tailored suits, chatted in groups, catching up on all the latest news. The women's bangles cascaded down their wrists as they danced with their partners beside the patio doors that opened on to the garden. But there was no sign of Mariam, thank goodness.

Mariam had better not ruin this party too, Zaiba thought. Zaiba knew that Samirah, another of her cousins, had spent months planning her Mehndi party. She'd wanted it to be the perfect party in the run-up to the perfect wedding, where Samirah – or Sam, as most people called her – would be the perfect bride. Sam liked perfect.

Zaiba relaxed a little and gave a sigh of pleasure – it was all so pretty! A Pakistani wedding was nothing without a Mehndi party beforehand, where the bride has parts of her body decorated in elaborate patterns with a red dye called henna. There would be choreographed dancing, special sweets fed to the bride and, importantly, her female relatives would share their advice for a happy marriage.

This party definitely had the three main ingredients for a successful Mehndi party in abundance – food, music and dancing! At the top of the room on a little stage was Sam. As the bride-to-be, she sat on a gilded white lounge chair, wearing a sari in deep red, orange and yellow. Zaiba saw her cousin stifle a yawn as she continued to sit patiently while her hands were decorated with the henna. Meanwhile her fiancé, Tanvir, had been cornered next to the punchbowl by some eager aunties who wanted to know *everything* about the upcoming wedding. It seemed at the moment that this party was fun for everyone *but* the young couple.

Zaiba felt a stab of sadness. Sam was her favourite cousin and Zaiba wanted this evening to be everything she'd hoped it would be. She glanced around the room, taking a mental note of as many details as possible. As the linen curtains swelled in the breeze, she noticed that the patio doors opened *out* on to the garden, rather than *in* to the room. That could be useful information if they were involved in a high-stakes chase! There was a main entrance leading out on to the drive too. She eased a little gold pencil that the receptionist had given her out of her bag and added extra details to the hotel map she'd drawn that morning. The receptionist – "Liza with a 'z'!" – had taken Zaiba and some of the other children round the hotel while their parents were busy unpacking. She'd pointed out the twenty-six bedrooms, the library with its leather-bound books and the extensive hotel grounds and separate buildings.

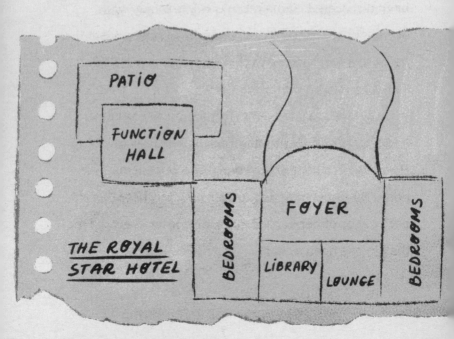

Zaiba opened the phone's voice recorder again and put it to her lips. "Observations: number of guests one, two, three, four, five . . . uhhhh, at least fifty people. Sofas and soft seating at ninety degrees to my right. Most people are on the dance floor. Bad – no *really* bad – music from the DJ booth close to the north-east window. No suspicious activity so far—"

"Apart from the girl hiding under the dining table!"

The tablecloth whipped up and a hand reached for Zaiba, pulling her swiftly out from her observation point.

"Aunt Fouzia!" Zaiba groaned, annoyed that she'd been discovered. Sam's mum was a tiny lady who somehow possessed the strength of a bodybuilder. Zaiba liked to imagine this strength came from all the extra-strong cups of chai Aunt Fouzia got through in a day – her record was ten! Zaiba quickly stashed away her phone, pencil and *Eden Lockett's Detective Handbook* in a little yellow purse she wore across her body. The hotel map was tucked carefully between the back pages of her book. A detective never knew when they might need a map!

"What are you doing sneaking about under there?" her aunt chided gently. "It's time for your family dance. And by the look on Samirah's face, she needs the entertainment. That henna artist is taking far too long!" Sam was Aunt Fouzia's eldest daughter and she was a doctor – "the youngest on her ward!" as Aunt Fouzia liked to remind people.

Zaiba had always looked up to Sam. She was clever and sophisticated and Zaiba often thought she could have been a spy if she'd wanted to be, like in the movies. She looked especially impressive today, if a little bit bored. As Zaiba glanced over at Samirah and Tanvir (or SamTan as Zaiba had decided their couple name was), she noticed the golden tikka hanging over Sam's forehead. It sparkled with rubies and sapphires, making Sam look like royalty.

"If I ever wear one of those, make sure I remember to hire a personal security team," Zaiba noted.

"Today the security is us," Aunt Fouzia teased. "Now come on, let's kick off this song and dance competition! Wait – where's Poppy?"

Poppy had been Zaiba's best friend for longer than she could remember. Since she was practically family she had been invited along to the party too. That morning Poppy's parents had dropped her off just in time for the tour of the hotel. Zaiba had lent Poppy one of her green silk dupattas to wear with her favourite party dress and Poppy had insisted on the matching green khussa. Parties involved two of Poppy's favourite things – dressing up and free food. Throw in a glamorous hotel and she was in heaven. This hotel in particular was right up her street. Liza had told them on their tour that it was built by some fancy-pants Lord ages ago. Zaiba thought he must have been a show-off since he had his home built like a mini castle, complete with three turrets that towered into the sky.

"Poppy! Over here!" Zaiba called, spotting her best friend over by a plate of brightly coloured burfi.

Poppy shoved the last sweet crumbs into her mouth and ran up to join Zaiba and a small group of children next to the dance floor.

Poppy linked her arm through Zaiba's as they

waited for three grannies to finish their routine to a famous Bollywood love song. "Did you complete your observations?" she asked Zaiba. "I was doing mine ... over by the chocolate fountain..."

Zaiba laughed. "I *was* doing them before Aunt Fouzia found me." She turned to her aunt. "How *did* you find me, by the way?"

"A great agent never reveals their secrets." Aunt Fouzia tapped the side of her nose. Zaiba's aunt was even more famous than Eden Lockett, in Karachi at least. She ran the **Snow Leopard Detective Agency** – the best agency in Pakistan. She'd encouraged Zaiba to read her first Eden Lockett mystery after Zaiba had asked one too many questions about Aunt Fouzia's job. Now Zaiba *and* Poppy were mega fans. Zaiba had Eden Lockett bed covers, Eden Lockett stationery... Aunt Fouzia had even found her an Eden Lockett phone case! Zaiba would call her aunt in Pakistan and they would talk for hours about their hero's latest adventure. Sometimes Zaiba thought that Aunt Fouzia loved the books even more than she did.

"She saw you because your feet were poking out!" Zaiba's younger half-brother Ali chimed in, wriggling between Zaiba and Poppy. "How long will we all have to dance until Sam's Mehndi is finished?"

"I heard you're top of your class in maths, Ali. How long do *you* think it will take?" Aunt Fouzia tested him.

Ali tapped a finger against his chin as he counted. "Hmmm, each hand would take around twenty minutes, then double that for the feet, plus drying time..."

"So, have you had any thrilling cases to solve recently, Auntie?" Zaiba asked, squeezing her aunt's hand while her brother's eyes darted around the room, making rapid calculations.

"You know I can't discuss any of my cases." Aunt Fouzia pursed her lips. "But let's just say, the prime minister owes me a big favour..."

"*The prime minister!*" the girls gasped. Aunt Fouzia was definitely the real deal. What could the crisis have been this time? Ten Bengal tigers let loose in parliament?

"... then the song and dance contest would have

to go on for one hour and fifty minutes!" said Ali triumphantly.

"Brilliant, Ali." Aunt Fouzia patted his cheek. "You'd better get dancing!"

The music for the grannies' dance finished and the whole room erupted into applause.

"Zaiba, Ali, there you are," came a warm voice from behind them. It was Zaiba's stepmum Jessica, who she called Mum, and she was ready to dance. "It's the moment we've been practising for!"

"I think I'll just watch this one, Mum." Zaiba wasn't much of a dancer, and besides, she couldn't keep up her safety observations and dance at the same time.

"What?" her mum cried. "But we've been working on it all week!" Zaiba's mum hadn't realized that the song and dance contest was supposed to be just a bit of fun. In fact she'd been taking it quite seriously, making the whole family stay up until late memorizing the choreography.

"I'll still perform, Mrs— Oh!" Poppy quickly shut up after Zaiba squeezed her hand.

But there wasn't time for Jessica to try and persuade them as the music had started and Zaiba's dad, Hassan, whisked Ali and Jessica on to the dance floor.

"Let's see those feet dancing," he grinned, shaking his hips to the beat.

2
WHO HAS A SECRET?

Zaiba glanced over at Sam, who was doing her best to stifle her laughter. Hassan's dad dancing had certainly cheered her up and her shoulders were shaking with laughter.

"Stop moving!" the henna artist scolded her. "Do you want a flower pattern or a squashed snail?" An important part of the Mehndi design was the inclusion of the husband's initials. Zaiba had heard stories that the longer the henna stain lasted on the bride's hands, the longer their love would last. But after hearing Zaiba's couple name suggestion, Sam had asked for *SamTan* to be written instead.

Zaiba's gaze returned to the dance floor. There was something about this that wasn't ... quite ... right.

"Dad doesn't normally dance," she muttered.

"You're lucky," Poppy said. "My dad dances in the kitchen all the time. It's so embarrassing!"

Zaiba tapped a finger against her chin, thinking. Why was her dad suddenly so interested in shaking his stuff on the dance floor in front of all these people? He'd sat watching cricket when they'd been practising at home. Dancing just wasn't him!

"Anyway, *I* wanted to dance..." Poppy pouted sulkily, drawing Zaiba's attention back to her best friend.

"Don't worry, Pops." Zaiba smiled. "I have a feeling Aunt Fouzia has found us something better to do." She looked up at her aunt whose eyes were scanning the room.

Aunt Fouzia cleared her throat and put on a deep voice. "I do indeed. Your next assignment, Agent Zaiba, with the assistance of Agent Poppy, is to work out..." She took Zaiba by the shoulders and steered her round to look at the rest of the room. "Who here has a secret. Let's see if you can read the body language of the guests."

Zaiba felt her detective skills kicking in. She immediately froze as she spotted Mariam still sitting silently with her parents. Mariam had been scowling at her nastily but her face broke out in a smug smile and she gave a thumbs down as she spotted Zaiba's dad dancing. He was kicking his feet like some sort of clumsy donkey! Zaiba's heart thumped in her chest. Did Mariam have to be quite so horrible to her still? Who carried that much of a grudge over a unicorn piñata?

As her cousin started to get down off her seat, Zaiba quickly looked away and searched the rest of the room. Aha! Grandpa's hand was creeping towards the last samosa on the buffet table. But before Zaiba could say anything, her grandma slapped his hand away. Well, Grandpa's big appetite wasn't such a big secret.

"Come on," Aunt Fouzia teased, poking Zaiba in the ribs. "Keep looking!"

Poppy had already given up and was watching the dancing, marking through the moves that she'd memorized the minute Zaiba had shown them to her. Zaiba concentrated harder. Could it be the sulky boy underneath the dining table using napkins to create a fort? *No*, that wouldn't be scandalous enough for her aunt Fouzia. She had to focus.

Focus.

"There!" Zaiba cried out, pointing at her suspect. She'd been right. Her dad *was* up to something!

"Shh!" Aunt Fouzia patted Zaiba on the head. "You've figured it out, but let's not ruin the surprise for the other guests."

Together they watched her dad sneak behind the curtains at the back of the dance floor and then pop out the other side to stand in a corner of the room. His gaze shifted from side to side. *What's he up to?* Zaiba wondered.

As Jessica, Ali and a few other cousins carried on dancing in formation, it was unlikely anyone would notice he was gone. Then a waiter with floppy hair, wearing a badly fitting uniform, appeared. He handed over a tray bearing a beautifully decorated celebration cake with multi-coloured-icing flowers piped around the edges to ... Zaiba's dad! *So that's what he was doing yesterday when he got up at 4am!* He'd told the family it was to watch the hockey – to watch the live matches in Pakistan, a fan had to get up extremely early. Last night's hockey had clearly been a cover story for her dad's other passion – baking.

He made an entire cake without me noticing, Zaiba thought glumly. "I can't believe I missed that."

"Don't worry." Her aunt gave her a hug. "Keep honing your detective skills. You'll get there!"

Suddenly a huge sigh of *ooohs* and *aaahhs* swept over the crowd. Zaiba's dad had reappeared on the dance floor holding out the celebration cake to SamTan. Everyone applauded and Sam blew them a kiss from the stage. Hassan carefully carried the cake over to her.

"Let's go get a closer look!" Poppy gushed, eyeing up the cake.

There was a pause as the music faded back into the DJ's own mix of cheesy pop. During the silence, Zaiba heard some banging above the ceiling. What was that? But Aunt Fouzia and Poppy each took hold of a hand and dragged her to join the small crowd up on the stage, who were admiring the celebration cake.

"Zaiba! Wasn't your family amazing?" Sam smiled.

"They were definitely ... astonishing," Zaiba joked, poking her tongue out at her dad.

"Are you enjoying the party?" Tanvir joined in.

"Oh, definitely. Thank you for inviting us!"

Poppy followed suit. "Happy wedding ... marriage ... thing," she stammered, handing Sam a present.

"Oh, Poppy, how sweet of you!" Sam was shocked. "You don't usually give the bride a present at a Mehndi so I really wasn't expecting anything..."

"And Pops ... that's a *pakora*," Zaiba whispered.

"Oops!" Poppy quickly swapped the snack for the small tissue-paper parcel she had tucked away in her purse.

"Poppy, it's beautiful!" Sam seemed touched as she opened the present. Inside was a beaded bracelet that Poppy had made at after-school club.

"And pakoras are my favourite." Tanvir winked, which made Poppy giggle.

"You must be over the moon." Jessica smiled, hugging Aunt Fouzia. "The party is wonderful and *such* a beautiful venue. A real-life castle for your princess!"

"Thank you, we were starting to lose hope at the end of last month. We couldn't seem to find anywhere to host us." Aunt Fouzia shrugged. "All the hotels in the area are having issues at the moment. No one would let us book! One hotel was flooded, one had a bug infestation. Then Mr Stevens at the White Hall cancelled last minute—"

"The Royal Star is beautiful!" Zaiba's dad chimed in, trying to cut off Aunt Fouzia's ramblings. "Just as beautiful as my niece!"

"Yes, but..." Sam began to say, placing a hand on Zaiba's shoulder.

"*And* did you know she's the youngest doctor on her ward?" Aunt Fouzia interrupted.

"Why, of course," Jessica replied.

"How could we ever forget?" Zaiba's dad added cheekily.

Zaiba cleared her throat. "I think Sam wanted to say something."

The bride kissed her on the cheek. "Thank you, Zaiba. What I was going to say is that I was a little nervous about how today would go."

"Why?" Zaiba asked, sensing a mystery.

"Well..." Sam started, tilting her head to one side, "the hotel manager phoned me last night to say that they had another last-minute guest for an event." She leaned into the group and they crowded round. "A celebrity!" She straightened up, smoothing down her silk sari. "I didn't want anything to take away from my day, but the hotel manager assured me that the hotel was all set up to cater for two important guests." She glanced at Tanvir. "Well, three important guests."

Zaiba's eyes widened. *A VIP guest, here?*

"Who's the celebrity?" she asked breathlessly.

Sam shrugged. "I don't know. It's confidential."

"We should go and investigate," Zaiba said to Poppy, who nodded eagerly.

Jessica turned to the girls. "Go on then, you two. But make sure you keep checking in with one of us."

Sam opened her arms and Zaiba gave her a big squeeze – being careful not to smudge her henna patterns that were still drying. One smudge and a whole flower design could be obliterated!

"It's going to be a great party," she whispered to her cousin. But looking up at Sam, Zaiba thought she could still see a glint of worry in her eyes. Zaiba knew that the surprise mystery guest wasn't the only reason Sam was feeling nervous.

Two days earlier Sam had confided in her younger cousin. "All those people, I'm not used to the attention being on me," she'd admitted, busily sorting through the personalized place settings. "What if I say something silly or trip over my dress?"

Zaiba felt a shiver of concern. Sam deserved the best Mehndi party in the world. She made a secret promise to herself that she would make *certain* Sam enjoyed her night.

"Don't worry, cuz," Zaiba said. "I'll make sure there's no funny business!"

"Zai, I think Poppy's waiting for you," her dad called, pointing towards the door where Poppy had already stationed herself. Zaiba quickly nodded and released Sam from her tight hug. But before Zaiba had a chance to follow her friend, her dad took her to one side and said seriously, "Zaiba, promise me you'll behave. It's a big deal for your cousin to have her party here."

"Of course." Zaiba crossed her heart.

Hassan chucked Zaiba under the chin. "Oh, and take your brother with you!" her parents sang together before disappearing back into the crowd.

"Look, Zaiba!" Ali tugged at his sister's sleeve.

Poppy was waving urgently from the doorway that led out on to the driveway. The Mehndi party was in the function hall of the hotel, a separate annexe just off from the reception area. Was the VIP guest here *already*?

"Go, sweetheart. See what you can detect!" Aunt Fouzia gave Zaiba a gentle push.

Zaiba raced across the dance floor, dodging couples and the waiter with floppy hair, who was now handing out drinks. She nearly ran into Mariam, who appeared out of nowhere to block her way.

"Where do you think you're going?" she asked, smiling smugly.

"Sorry, Mariam. I just need to get past," Zaiba panted,

ducking to one side. She really didn't want another argument now. Ali raced past them to the door, looking back at Mariam curiously.

"I knew your family would make fools of themselves in the dance contest," Mariam laughed nastily and wiggled her phone at Zaiba. "Now I'll *always* have video evidence. Who shall I send it to first? How about ... everyone in your year group at school?"

Zaiba sighed impatiently. "Do what you want. But don't forget, Mariam, they're *your* family too."

She continued on past her cousin – now standing in stunned silence – towards Poppy, who was still frantically waving. If anyone was going to get a first look at the celebrity, it was definitely going to be Pops!

3
AGENTS ASSEMBLE

Zaiba peeped out of the annexe's front doorway on to the grand driveway of the hotel. An intricately carved stone fountain sprayed water into the air, the droplets sparkling in the sun. On their tour of the hotel, Liza the receptionist had explained that the function hall used to be a barn and that's why it was separate to the main building. This was probably for the best since Uncle Zaid had just started up the karaoke machine...

"I can see why it's called the *Royal* Star – the queen could live here!" Zaiba gazed in awe at the three turrets. The building was split into three main sections – each leading up to a turret straight out of a fairy tale.

The middle section was the largest, where the hotel lobby was. This had one tall turret that looked out over the gardens, which surrounded the hotel in glossy, manicured lawns.

"That's definitely where I'd want to live if I was a princess," Poppy laughed, pointing at the spindly tower.

Two muscular men in black suits had positioned themselves by the main entrance's revolving door and were engaged in a walkie-talkie conversation with an unseen person. They looked like bodyguards from a film!

"OK, agents, easy does it," commanded Zaiba as they pushed their way through the revolving door, past the men and into the lobby. Zaiba put her hand up to signal a pause.

"I don't see any celebrity," Poppy huffed. Hotel staff were hurrying about and a handful of guests were checking out. A maid was dusting the heavy oak reception desk as two men in uniforms kicked out a long roll of red carpet across the tiled floor. Everything was polished to a high shine.

"They can't have arrived yet. But I definitely want to be

here when they do! Let's stay inside, out of sight. We can go to the window and take a closer look."

Zaiba crept over to it, beckoning the others to follow her.

"This is the fanciest place I've ever been," Poppy whispered. "I can see my face in that doorknob!"

The main hotel looked like one of those old black and white films that Zaiba's mum liked to watch at the weekend. The walls were a dark maroon colour and the tiled floor was chequered black and white. Hanging on the walls were imposing oil paintings of old wrinkly men. It all seemed very familiar...

She gasped. "It's just like the place described in *The Hidden Staircase*," Zaiba whispered to Poppy. Aunt Fouzia had told Zaiba that Eden Lockett had stayed at this actual hotel and it had inspired her to write her sixth novel. Zaiba had no idea how someone wrote six whole novels – and that wasn't even counting the others she'd written after the books had become an international success! But Eden Lockett had, all about her crime-fighting adventures.

"Here we go with Eden Lockett!" Ali said, rolling his eyes. Zaiba's brother liked to pretend he was too cool for detective missions but she knew he liked helping. No, loved helping!

"But she's a brilliant detective," Poppy retorted.

Zaiba grinned. "A secret agent."

"A genius!"

"The ultimate ..."

"... super spy!"

The girls high-fived in honour of their favourite hero.

"But how does Aunt Fouzia know that Eden Lockett stayed here? Does she know who Eden is?" Poppy pondered out loud. It was known among fans that Eden Lockett was just a pen name for a mystery author.

"She wouldn't tell me," Zaiba recalled unhappily. "She just tapped her nose like she always does." Zaiba was certain that getting answers from a world-class agent like Aunt Fouzia would *not* be easy.

Suddenly there was a noise from beyond the windows. "Look, over there," Zaiba whispered, pointing. An enormous shiny car was pulling up in the hotel's drive.

"It's a limousine! Come on, let's get a closer look. Agents assemble!"

They rushed to the window seat and clambered up among the cushions – Zaiba in the middle, Poppy on her right-hand side and Ali perched on the edge. Zaiba slipped her phone out of her purse and began a voice recording.

"Time: 16:00 hours. Clue one – the hotel porter is rushing to open the door for the guest. He did not do this for us."

"That's because we're only kids," Ali pointed out.

"Shh, Ali!" Zaiba did her best to ignore her brother. "Clue two: the canine. Looks pedigree. I think it's a—"

"Italian greyhound!" Poppy said in a rush. They were her favourite breed. A tiny little grey dog flopped out of the limousine on to the gravel, stretching its back legs. It was wearing a little quilted jacket and a sparkling collar with a charm at its throat.

"A dog like that is seriously expensive," Poppy said, her eyes wide.

"*How* expensive?" Zaiba asked.

Poppy shrugged. "An Italian greyhound can cost—"

"Anywhere between five hundred and two thousand pounds," Ali interrupted. For the millionth time, Zaiba wondered how her little brother kept all these facts and figures in his head. He shuffled forwards on the window seat, his nose pressed against the glass. "But they could just be rich, rather than a celebrity."

"And clue number three..." Zaiba turned back to her phone and gestured at the endless stream of people arriving. There was someone carrying the celebrity's handbag, another person clutching a mobile phone to her ear and a man in a black suit who shifted a zipped protective clothes cover on his shoulder, the bag bulging with outfits. "She's travelling with an entourage. That's definitely a celebrity move."

"How do you know it's a woman?" Poppy asked.

Zaiba gestured to the limousine's door. A pair of elegant feet in shiny red shoes appeared.

"Correlis!" Poppy burst out. Zaiba had no idea what this meant, but Poppy's passion for fashion suggested she was talking about the high heels.

"Look, I bet that woman's her assistant." Zaiba pointed at a young woman with blond hair slicked back into a neat bun. "Can you see her in-ear headset and the way she's bossing the others around? She must be the one giving instructions to the men at the door."

The celebrity's entourage swarmed around the limousine. One of the muscular men stepped forwards from his position in the doorway with a large umbrella to shield the celebrity from view. A clever tactic! Zaiba got her phone ready to take some pictures for evidence, steadying her elbows on the window frame.

Now all they needed was for that umbrella to move *just a bit lower...*

"Curiosity killed the cat," purred a voice. Zaiba whirled round to see a man standing behind them. He wore a waistcoat with a pocket watch on a chain and rocked back and forth on his heels. It was the hotel manager, Mr Ainsley. They'd bumped into him earlier, when Liza had been explaining how the hotel chandeliers each had three hundred and thirteen crystals.

"*Three hundred and fourteen* crystals," a bald man in an

immaculate suit had interrupted. "I would never have three hundred and thirteen crystals in a chandelier – everyone knows that the number thirteen is bad luck."

"Sorry, sir," Liza had said meekly. "I was just showing our new guests around."

"Ah, part of the Mehndi party," Mr Ainsley had replied with a stiff bow. Zaiba had never had a person bow to her before. "We are honoured." He'd turned away towards the library, but as he passed Liza he'd leaned close to give her a last instruction. "Remember, the VIP suite above the function room is still having the sunken jacuzzi put in. No one's to go there. Those plumbers will be the death of me. They've already lost one gold tap." And then he'd marched off, shutting the library door behind him.

Now, Mr Ainsley didn't look very "honoured" any more to see them. "Little girls should no—" he began to say.

"And boy!" Ali protested.

"*And boy*," Mr Ainsley corrected himself. "Should not be snooping on our distinguished guests. Come on, come away from the window." He helped them down and ushered them across the hotel lobby, back towards the annexe and the Mehndi party. There was a side door leading straight off the lobby into a corridor that attached to the annexe. Why hadn't Zaiba noticed this before? She'd have to add that detail to her map later. The side door stood ajar and Zaiba could see a pair of glittering eyes watching them. *Mariam again!* She must have told Mr Ainsley that they were snooping.

"I think they're about to do a conga line, you wouldn't want to miss that." Mr Ainsley interrupted Zaiba's thoughts.

The hotel manager walked towards his office, adjusting his crisp black blazer. His hands fiddled with the buttons and Zaiba noticed diamond cufflinks twinkling at the wrists. The office door had a brass nameplate reading *Hotel Manager*. As Mr Ainsley flung it open, Zaiba saw a little shelf with neat rows of tiny crystalline figures and awards the hotel had won. *Wow*, she thought. *He really likes glittery things.*

On the shelf below was another collection. A shamrock, a horseshoe, some dice and a little pottery ladybird.

"That's a random collection! What are they for?" whispered Ali.

But Zaiba knew immediately. She thought back to the twelfth Eden Lockett novel, *The Case of the Charm*. "They're lucky charms," she whispered back. "Mr Ainsley clearly is superstitious."

"Or really desperate for the hotel to succeed," Ali suggested. "Doesn't he know that's all nonsense?"

"Maybe he's both," Poppy added. "Superstitious *and* desperate for the hotel to succeed."

Just as he was about to shut his office door, Liza called over to him. "Mr Ainsley, it's the kitchen. Apparently the sandwiches have been cut into squares instead of triangles."

Mr Ainsley sighed and went over to the reception desk. "Oh, that won't do! I've told them a thousand times that sandwiches at the Royal Star only *ever* have three sides." He shook his head despairingly. "We already have an issue with the VIP suite. I don't need any more headaches today!" As he passed, rubbing his brow, he gave Zaiba and the others one last warning look.

"Remember. You're welcome to explore the hotel, but leave our guests their privacy." Then he glided away.

"It's like he's on wheels or something," Poppy muttered.

The revolving door wheezed round. The celebrity and her entourage were making their way into the lobby. Zaiba gestured to a tall pot plant in the corner. "Quick! Over here!"

The three of them ran to hide. Zaiba held a finger to her lips before they carefully peered out. What would they see? A manicured hand waving? A shake of a famous head of curls? But there were too many people blocking the view! The only thing Zaiba could make out was the snout of the Italian greyhound as it sniffed around people's feet on the red carpet.

Mr Ainsley rushed to greet the celebrity and then knelt to stroke the dog. His hand drifted to the charm at its collar.

"Ah!" they heard him say with interest. "Is that a lucky charm?" He straightened up to lead the celebrity away and Zaiba peered round to see the charm. It was a crescent moon with a little star hanging from its tip.

"I can't see anything," Ali grumbled.

"Shh!" Zaiba and Poppy said in unison. Mr Ainsley was now scolding the doorman who had scuffed the celebrity's designer suitcase.

"Well, it *is* a Favelli Favello," Poppy whispered.

"What's that, a type of pasta? Let me see!" Ali started to push Zaiba out of the way.

"Stop shoving me," Zaiba hissed, shoving him back.

THUMP! Zaiba's elbow hit the wooden panelling of the back wall.

"Ow," she moaned, rubbing her arm. Then she froze. She stopped rubbing and started rapping her knuckles against the wall. "Did you hear that?" she whispered.

Poppy shrugged. "No?"

"Listen again." Zaiba tapped along the edges of each wooden panel, concentrating hard.

Thud... Thud... Thud... THUMP!

That fourth thump had definitely sounded different.

Poppy's eyes lit up with understanding. "Hollow," she whispered.

Zaiba stifled an excited squeal. This was just like when Eden Lockett discovered *The Hidden Staircase*! Could the staircase really exist?

"Let's see if this works..." Zaiba started to feel around the edges of the panel, looking for a hidden pressure point.

Ping!

The panel slid open.

"You're a genius!" breathed Poppy.

"Don't," Ali said. "It'll go to her head." But he did look impressed.

Zaiba switched on her phone torch and angled it into the dark corridor that was hidden behind the sliding panel. A cloud of thick dust hung in the air and cobwebs stretched across the entrance. She squinted to make out a series of steps, winding up the building.

She'd been waiting to find one of these her whole life.

"A secret staircase," she whispered, her eyes wide in amazement. "The very same one Eden Lockett wrote about."

"So it wasn't just make-believe," Poppy said in awe.

They heard the sudden ping of the lift doors closing. The mystery celebrity was getting away!

"Come on," Zaiba stepped boldly into the hidden corridor, pulling Poppy and Ali after her. When else would she get the chance to follow a secret staircase?

"This could allow us to explore the whole hotel..."

Poppy's face lit up. "Secretly!"

"So we can track down our prey," Ali said, grinning.

"She's not our prey," Zaiba corrected. "She's our mission."

Poppy's eyes gleamed. "Mission! I like it."

The three of them turned to peer up the gloomy stairs. Zaiba put her weight on the first step, testing it.

"Woah! I didn't think you'd actually go through with it," said Ali, shaking his head in admiration. "Especially with all those cobwebs... "

"*We*'re going through with it. Come on!" Zaiba replied, excited.

Poppy smiled, switching on the torch from her phone too. She and Zaiba shone their beams on

the dark narrow stairs, which wound upwards in
a corkscrew and out of sight. "We're going to catch
a celebrity!"

4
THE SECRET STAIRCASE

"Quick, Poppy. Close the panel!" The last thing they needed was Mr Ainsley halting their mission.

Poppy located an old brass knob on the inside of the panel and slid it shut, before turning to peer up at the old wooden staircase. "This is *so* cool," she said, clapping her hands together.

"Yeah ... really cool. If you're not afraid of spiders." Ali didn't seem so sure. Directly in front of him was a large spider's web the size of a frying pan! Zaiba knew spiders were her brother's biggest fear, so she took his hand.

"Don't worry," she reassured him. "They're more frightened of you than you are of them."

Ali didn't look convinced. "That's what people always say, but have you seen how big a Goliath birdeating tarantula can grow!"

"I'm pretty sure there aren't any of those here." At least she hoped there weren't.

The stairs looked like no one had used them for years. There was a thick layer of dust covering each step and cobwebs laced the bannisters.

Zaiba opened the voice recorder again. "The time is 16:15 hours," she said. "We are about to climb Eden Lockett's secret staircase!" A thrill of excitement at the sound of those words made her heart beat faster. "Let's go, team. Tread lightly!"

One by one, they climbed the twisting stairs, counting the steps as they went. Zaiba led the way, still squeezing Ali's hand. Poppy followed behind them. They made their way up a flight of stairs, each holding their breath in anticipation of what they might find.

"I know I said this before," Poppy started to say. "But this is so – a-a–a-ach-CHOO!"

"Oh my gosh!" Zaiba exclaimed.

"I'm sorry, I didn't mean to be so loud."

"No, look!" Zaiba shone her torch ahead. "It's a door."

She put her ear to the keyhole and heard muffled voices. Did any of them sound like a celebrity? It was hard to tell. She listened harder and heard something about "sink blocked" and "plunger". She was pretty sure that celebrities didn't unblock their own sinks. That sounded like cleaners.

Zaiba tried giving the door a push but it was jammed. Or locked. She spoke into her phone: "Time: 16:20 hours. A locked door on the first floor. We will continue up."

She noticed a couple of sets of footprints in the dust – a zigzag print and a print that looked like snakeskin – but before she could inspect them further Ali gave a shudder. "Can we just get away from these spiders ... quickly?"

Up the curling staircase they continued, following the light of Zaiba's phone. She prayed that any creepy-crawlies – or ghosts or vampires! – stayed hidden. Every time they reached a door they'd try it, but the doors were always locked. On the second floor there was an extra-big door but again it was locked.

"This is the floor our room's on," Ali mumbled, getting his bearings by spinning round in a small circle. "The staircase runs up the centre of the building, so..." He glanced at the door again and snapped his fingers, "that door must lead to the west wing, same wing as us."

Zaiba looked at her little brother in amazement, he was practically a human compass. "Great observations, Ali!"

"It might even be our room!" Poppy said. "We're on the second floor too."

"Hmmm." Zaiba looked at the door – it was wide and had a big brass handle. "There definitely isn't a door like this in our room." She put her ear to the door and could hear noises on the other side of the panels – hotel staff talking to each other as they tidied.

Eventually, they reached the very top of the staircase, which led to a final door that also led out on to the west wing of the hotel. Zaiba leaned against it and it swung open with a squeak of rusty hinges.

"Result!" Zaiba stepped through. "But this is definitely not a celebrity's suite."

As they wandered around, the floorboards creaked and groaned. They were in a large dingy room with sloping eaves that met in a point, like a tent. Pushed up against the wall were six iron bed frames that seemed to have been abandoned a long time ago. Zaiba opened the drawer of a faded old dresser, but there were no clues inside as to where they were. She felt Ali's hand grip hers tighter every time the floorboards squeaked and she squeezed it back gently.

"I think I've seen a place like this before..." Poppy strolled between the rows of small iron bed frames. She clicked her fingers. "I know! These must have been the servants' sleeping quarters. Like on the TV show I love, *Toffton Manor*."

"Great detective work, Poppy." Zaiba gave her best friend a high five before she returned to make another voice recording. "We have located old servant's quarters. Observations to follow." She turned off the phone.

At the top of the stairs Zaiba had hoped to find the penthouse suite where a celebrity might stay, but this couldn't be it. She certainly wouldn't be staying in an old forgotten servant's bedroom.

They could hear voices floating up from the room below and the bark of an ... Italian greyhound? The friends looked at each other, eyes shining with excitement.

"How do we find out who's down there?" Zaiba asked.

Ali glanced around the room, muttering to himself. He looked at the bare bulb that hung from the attic roof. "If there was a light fitting there, then there must be another one in the same place in the room below. Rooms are usually wired in the same way."

Zaiba stared at her little brother. "How do you know how rooms are wired?"

He shrugged. "I watch a lot of video tutorials online."

Sure enough, directly below the light fitting was a hole in the floorboards where another light fitting must have been once upon a time. Zaiba glanced up at Poppy and Ali.

"A spyhole!" Zaiba said in a whisper. She shoved her phone in a pocket and put a finger to her lips, warning the others to stay quiet. Then she lay down, lowered her face to the hole and peered through. Success! They were right above a room with a deep, luxurious carpet. She pressed her face closer to the hole and looked again. Standing directly beneath her was a young woman with shockingly bright red hair.

I recognize that colour! Oh my goodness, this could be big, she thought, not daring to make a sound.

In the celebrity's arms a dog was nuzzling into her shoulder. It was the Italian greyhound! He really was a cute dog. A manicured hand stroked his glossy grey coat. He suddenly cocked an ear, listening to something. Zaiba's breathing? She tried to stay very still against the floorboards.

The woman with red hair was lit from all sides by a circle of tall lights on stands. It looked like a photo shoot. This was the celebrity all right! Who else would receive so much attention?

"Who IS it?" Poppy whispered.

"I still can't see her face," Zaiba replied.

The celebrity moved to sit in a chair opposite another person with a microphone. There was the sound of a pencil scribbling on paper. A journalist! The celebrity was being interviewed as well as being photographed. *Snap, snap, snap!*

"So what made you decide to move from TV to film?" the journalist asked in a low, smooth voice.

Zaiba wiggled around, trying to see the celebrity's face. *She's here to promote a film?* This was getting more exciting by the moment!

The celebrity was trying to answer but the Italian greyhound was getting restless, shuffling in her arms.

"Here, take Roberto, will you?" she asked an unseen assistant. "And don't let him off his lead."

That voice! It was instantly recognizable. Zaiba had been listening to it every week for the past year. That hair colour, that voice and the special way she rolled her 'r's... Zaiba started to sit back on her heels when – wait! Who else could she see? She pressed her other eye to the hole this time.

Zaiba saw a pair of hands reach out and Roberto was handed over. *Roberto... A fancy name for a fancy dog!* The celebrity crossed her legs. Zaiba's curiosity set her heart beating. She switched her other eye to the tiny spyhole, hoping to get a different perspective, but now she could only see someone sitting by some French windows that opened out on to a balcony. Beyond, she could see Mr Ainsley and the waiter with floppy hair who Zaiba recognized from the Mehndi party. They were adjusting some teacups on a tray. Roberto had curled up by the French windows, basking in the sunshine. He shifted and something caught the sunlight, glinting even more brightly than his collar.

"Wow," Zaiba exclaimed. "That charm on his collar – it's a huge diamond." She leaned back and rubbed her eyes. "The sparkle's so bright!"

"I want to see." Zaiba shuffled aside and Poppy put her eye to the spyhole. She gasped. "Wow, the glare is so bright that I can hardly see anything!"

As Poppy peered down, Zaiba noticed a sound coming from the stairwell. The creak of a floorboard and then the rusty wheeze of hinges as someone stepped into the room.

"Mariam!" Poppy gulped. "What are you doing here?"

"I could ask you the same question." Mariam folded her arms and looked them up and down.

Poppy and Zaiba shared a panicked glance. The last time they'd been alone with Mariam with no adults nearby was a nightmare. Mariam had held Zaiba's Eden Lockett pencil case for ransom unless Zaiba swapped her SuperSplasher 3.0 birthday present for Mariam's SuperSplasher 2.0. Zaiba always seemed to end up with better birthday presents than Mariam, but that wasn't her fault! No way did she want Mariam taking anything again. In fact, it was only because Sam had stepped in that Zaiba got her pencil case back in one piece.

Mariam gazed around the attic. "I'm waiting... Are you going to tell me what you're doing up here? Or shall I go and get the hotel manager right now?"

Zaiba patted her little yellow bag to make sure *Eden Lockett's Detective Handbook* was safely tucked away. "Nothing. Just..."

"It's none of your business!" Ali burst out, his face red. He knew how unhappy Mariam had made Zaiba, but she wished he could be a little less obvious about how much they disliked their cousin. It would only make Mariam even more nasty.

"You're doing one of your stupid Eden Lockett missions again, aren't you?" Mariam laughed nastily. "I remember you getting grounded last time we were at Nana's house for snooping!"

"Only because you told her to come outside exactly when we were climbing the neighbour's fence!" Zaiba was losing her patience. No one called Eden Lockett stupid on her watch.

"Besides, we're not snooping. You are." Ali took a protective step in front of Zaiba.

"Ssh, Ali," Zaiba whispered to him. "I can handle this."

Mariam dropped her glance down to the hem of Zaiba's dress. "Oh dear. Aunt Jessica won't be happy."

Zaiba looked down and saw – oh no! – she'd torn her dress. The dress that had been bought especially for the wedding. The dress that her mum had told her to take care of.

"Don't—" She looked back up at Mariam but it was too late. She had already clattered away down the stairs.

"She followed us," Poppy said, shaking her head. "*She's* the snoop!"

"I know," Zaiba said. "But we can't let her get in the way of our mission."

She dropped to the floor for one last look through the spyhole. Just as Zaiba put her eye to the hole, she saw a pair of hands reach down and unclip the lead from Roberto's collar.

"The celebrity said not to do that," Zaiba muttered to herself.

"Not to do what?" Ali asked impatiently, trying to budge Zaiba over.

"Take the dog off its lead, now SHH!" Zaiba pushed him away firmly.

The greyhound had settled back down by the French windows. As she watched, something hit Zaiba. The view from the balcony was of the back gardens. She could just make out a line of oak trees – the same oak trees she'd seen from the balcony in the room she was sharing with Poppy. Their *shared* balcony, on the floor below. Oh my goodness!

Zaiba quickly got up and dusted herself off. "Come on, guys," she whispered. "We have to go to our room – now!"

"Thank goodness." Ali shuddered. "I've counted thirteen spiders up here – and that's not including the dead ones."

"But what about our mission?" Poppy protested.

"It's about to be completed with any luck." Zaiba smiled, heading for the door. "Our celebrity might be staying right next door to us!"

5
UNDER THE SPOTLIGHT

Zaiba hurried out on to the dusty staircase with the others following close behind. Dark shadows gathered in the corners as the attic door creaked shut behind them. Zaiba lifted her hand before her face and could barely make out the outline of her fingers, before switching on her phone torch. She gave a shudder and thought that Mariam must have been quite brave, creeping up the secret staircase all on her own.

"But why would a celebrity be in a room next door to us?" Ali asked. "She's a *celebrity*! And Mum and Dad got that room on special offer."

Zaiba paused and looked at Poppy. "Can you think

why?" she asked, letting her friend practise her detective skills. She was so proud of her own deductions, she could almost burst!

Poppy shrugged. "She likes roughing it?"

Ali's eyes widened. "Don't let Dad hear you say that. He's super excited about the bidet in our bathroom."

Zaiba rolled her eyes. "Where do celebrities normally stay?"

Poppy thrust her hand into the air, as though she was answering a question at school. "In luxury penthouse suites! I know that from my *Kewl!* magazine."

"Oh yes!" cried Ali. "But a penthouse suite would be on the top floor and here there's just an attic." He stared down the stairs.

"So where else in the hotel could there be a luxury suite on the top floor?" Zaiba prompted him.

Ali snapped his fingers. "Mr Ainsley talked about the VIP suite on top of the function hall, remember!"

"That's right. Well done, Ali. Your detective instincts are really coming on. I definitely heard some banging up there between the music. Sounded like repairs."

Poppy gave a little jig of excitement. "The celebrity can't stay in the VIP suite because it's being repaired. She had to stay in the room next to ours because she had no choice! Because—"

"Because she was a last-minute guest in the hotel," Zaiba finished. "The hotel asked Sam if she was all right with two important guests. Come on, this mission is hotting up!"

The three of them began to run back down the stairs.

"Do you think anyone will know that we've been up here?" Ali asked, a frown creasing his brow.

"Not if we left everything as we found it," Zaiba told him. "We did leave everything exactly as we found it, didn't we?"

Ali and Poppy shared a glance. "Yes...?"

But it was too late to turn back now. "I don't think anyone comes up here, not even the hotel staff. Look!" Zaiba stopped abruptly and ran a finger over the bannister, which ended up covered with grey fluff. The others stumbled into the back of her.

She looked down at their footprints in the dust, tracing a path up the stairs. Mariam must have followed the track up here. But now they'd been scuffed away by the other girl's hasty exit.

Finally they reached the sliding-panel door. Zaiba dug her fingernails beneath a panel and gently eased it open, ushering Poppy and Ali through before herself. This was Eden Lockett's golden rule number five: *A good agent always ensures the safety of her friends.* She took one last look at the secret staircase before easing the door shut. With an almost silent *click!* it locked back in place. She smoothed a hand over the polished wooden surface. No one would know the secret passage was there.

"Amazing," her brother whispered.

"It is," she agreed. "I'm almost sad to leave it—"

"Um, Earth to Zaiba," Poppy interrupted. "We have a celebrity to track down, remember!"

Zaiba checked her watch. At about half past five the traditional part of the ceremony where Samirah's female relatives fed her Pakistani sweets would begin. Zaiba realized she had better get back to the party before that happened. If they missed that part of the Mehndi party, they'd be in Aunt Fouzia's bad books for a long time!

"I think we'd better go round the back of the hotel to our room," she said. "We don't want to meet anyone we know on the main stairs. But we need to be quick!"

Zaiba, Poppy and Ali ran across the polished marble floor and burst out of the hotel's entrance into the fading sunlight, their feet crunching on the gravel as they skirted the side of the hotel. There was a narrow path lit by fairy lights that led the way round to the part of the hotel where their rooms were. There was a separate, smaller entrance on this side of the hotel – away from the annexe where some the guests might have moved outside.

Zaiba raised her finger to her lips and opened the door. They stepped inside, their feet sinking into thick carpet that would silence the heaviest step. Perfect! They ran up the stairs and plunged into their corridor, counting down the door numbers as they passed each hotel room.

"12, 14 ... 15! Hold on, what?" Zaiba went back to count again. There was no room number 13. "Wow, Mr Ainsley really doesn't like the number thirteen."

She shrugged and took the room key from her yellow purse to let them in to the room where she and Poppy were staying. Ali had to sleep on the little cot bed in his parent's room – much to his dismay. Inside, they switched on the light and—

"Oh no!" Poppy pointed at the hem of Zaiba's dress.

"What? What's wrong?" Zaiba swished her shalwar kameez, trying to see. Had a Goliath birdeating spider or a mouse run under her skirts?

"It ... it's your dress!" Poppy stuttered.

Ali sighed. "Oh for goodness sake, Poppy. I thought something awful had happened!"

Zaiba's hands stilled and she looked more closely at her dress. Now, in addition to the rip that zigzagged along the hem, it was covered in dust and filthy streaks of dirt. She glanced up at her friends. Ali and Poppy's party clothes didn't look much better.

Ali's shirt was hanging out and one of his sleeves was torn, while Poppy had a cobweb sticking to her shoulder and her tulle underskirt was sagging and torn around the edges. Their parents would not be happy!

"Here!" Zaiba went into the bathroom and grabbed a hand towel, passing it to Poppy. "Brush yourself down and take off your underskirt." She ran some water over a facecloth and wrung it out, then began dabbing at her own dress. "We'll get rid of the worst of it. Ali, tuck your shirt in and dust yourself off. We're close to finding and identifying that celebrity!" Zaiba knew who the celebrity was from that bright-red hair and lilting voice but she wanted to see what Ali and Poppy thought, without influencing their opinions.

Ali shoved his shirt into his trousers, not looking very happy. "I don't know why I couldn't have worn my favourite hoody," he grumbled. "Then I wouldn't have had to worry about staying neat and tidy."

Zaiba rolled her eyes. "Even I know you don't wear a hoody to a Mehndi party. Follow me." Zaiba led them over to the room's large French windows, looking out over a small balcony. She peered round. A trellis wall separated their room from the next-door suite, where there was a matching set of French windows. They must lead into the celebrity's room!

Ali and Poppy craned to look through the holes of the trellis while Zaiba stood on a chair to try and see over.

"We won't see anything through this fence," Poppy sighed, sinking on to a chair.

"We're still too far away. I bet we could peep through the curtains, if we could just get close enough..." Zaiba paused, looking excited.

Ali's eyes lit up with understanding. "You wouldn't!"

"I would," Zaiba told her little brother.

Zaiba took out her phone. "The time is 17:00 hours," she whispered into the voice recorder. "We are crossing over on to the target's balcony."

A smile spread across Poppy's face. "Awesome!"

Ali was already rolling up his trouser cuffs.

"No, you stay here as lookout." Zaiba put a hand on his shoulder. "Warn us if our parents come up."

"Oh, Zaiba!" His shoulders sagged dramatically.

"Oh, Zaiba, nothing. We NEED a lookout and you're it."

Sulkily, Ali stomped over to the hotel door and peered out through the tiny spyhole in the wood. "Newsflash: Nothing."

"Are you sure it's not rude to peep on the celebrity?" Poppy asked as they prepared to climb the fence.

"That's a good question." Zaiba paused. "I think if the celebrity has left the curtains open, then it's OK to peep. But if the curtains are closed, then we should respect their privacy."

"Really?" Ali groaned from the doorway.

"*Really*."

One after the other, Zaiba and Poppy scrambled over the fence, using the holes in the trellis like a ladder. It wasn't too high and they were over in no time.

Zaiba jabbed a finger at the French windows and motioned for Poppy to follow. There was a nook in the corner of the balcony that was far away enough from the window that they wouldn't be spotted, but close enough to peek in. Huddled together on the floor, the girls peered through the glass. The curtains had been left ajar – success!

Zaiba caught a glimpse of someone inside the room. She saw ... a lock of glossy hair, a silk blouse, perfectly painted red lips, smiling. It was ... it was...

"It's Maysoon! From *Swing Sing!*" Poppy gushed, trying to keep her voice to a whisper. "This was definitely worth getting my dress ruined for." Immediately, Poppy began humming a song. "Do you recognize it? It's Maysoon's hit single. It's number one in the charts!"

"I do, but shh," Zaiba warned. "We're still on the mission, remember?"

Concentrating hard, Zaiba scanned the room, trying to remember every detail. *An agent's information is only as good as their memory,* Eden Lockett had written in *The Case of the Golden Egg*.

A crowd of people filled the suite. In the centre of it all Maysoon perched on a chair, spotlights trained on her. It must have been hot beneath their glare and the singer's cheeks seemed a little flushed. She was fiddling with her necklace as she answered questions from a journalist. The journalist had short clipped hair and very thick black arched eyebrows. Zaiba thought he looked like he was perpetually shocked. Roberto sat at Maysoon's feet and his glossy flanks gave a huge sigh as he settled his nose on his paws. *That dog looks really bored*, Zaiba thought.

Now that two detectives had identified Maysoon, Zaiba focused on the other activity in the room. She watched as a chef brought in a trolley covered in plates of food and bottles of water. The woman with the blond hair in a bun that they had seen earlier subtly handed the man a crisp fifty-pound note. *That's strange*, Zaiba thought. *I thought celebrities didn't have to pay for anything*.

"And how are you *really* feeling about this next chapter in your career?" asked the journalist, staring hard at Maysoon from behind a pair of thick black glasses. "Don't you think it's a risk? After all, you're a TV judge and singer, *not* an actor."

Maysoon let out an exasperated sigh, tapping the glass face of her designer watch. "I said only six questions." She raised herself up on the chair to peer past the journalist. "Aren't we finished yet, Georgia?"

The blond woman looked up. *So she is the PA!* Zaiba noticed her twitch with alarm and glance around the room. *She seems nervous*, Zaiba noted.

The journalist furrowed his brows and held the bridge of his nose with a thumb and forefinger.

"Either the journalist isn't happy with Maysoon *or* he has a bad headache," Zaiba whispered to Poppy.

Georgia the PA clapped her hands together. "Right! Everyone. Let's give Maysoon a break and some fresh air. Now, please!" She pushed through the crowd and began to head towards...

"Oh no! She's coming to open the French windows!" Zaiba jerked back and grabbed Poppy's hand. "Quickly! If they find us, we'll probably get kicked out of the hotel and ruin Sam's Mehndi party!"

The girls scrambled from their hiding place and headed for the fence, Zaiba helping Poppy across before clambering over herself.

"Quick, Zaiba, come on!" Poppy beckoned Zaiba through the open French windows and they threw themselves into their room *just* before they heard Maysoon's door open.

Poppy collapsed on the bed, panting.

"Well, who is it?" Ali looked from Poppy to a red-faced Zaiba.

"Who was what?" came a voice from the door.

"Ali, I told you to keep watch!" Zaiba hissed.

Mariam had poked her head round the door that Ali had left ajar and now came sliding in, observing the scene before her.

"Why are your cheeks all red? Only guilty people blush when they've been caught making trouble." Mariam jabbed a finger at Poppy's face.

"Stop following us! Don't you have anything better to do?" Ali pouted.

"Actually I do." Mariam lifted her chin and looked at Zaiba. "It's time for the family to feed Sam the sweets and she was sad you weren't there. So I offered to come and get you." Mariam smiled an angelic smile – but it wasn't fooling Zaiba.

"I bet she wouldn't have been so sad if you hadn't pointed it out." But Zaiba couldn't help but feel a pang of guilt in her tummy. "OK, team," she said, turning to Poppy and Ali. "Let's head back to the party."

"Do we get some of the sweets too?" Poppy asked, smoothing down her skirt as best she could.

Zaiba ignored her and turned back to Mariam.

"You go first."

With her chin held high Mariam headed back out in the hallway humming a self-satisfied little tune to herself.

"But who's the celebrity—" Ali began to whisper.

"We'll tell you on the way," Zaiba said in a low voice as they headed out of the room and into the corridor. They had to be there in time for Sam's special moment!

6
THE GREAT ESCAPE

The sound of bhangra music grew louder as the trio hurried through the gardens of the hotel towards the patio doors of the function hall. Mariam had already disappeared back inside as Zaiba hung back for a debrief with Poppy and Ali.

"I can't believe Maysoon is staying at the same place as us!" Poppy said, racing along behind Zaiba. "And Sam said it was last minute because they couldn't find another hotel – we're so lucky!"

"How exactly are they going to make a *Swing Sing* movie?" Ali was doing his best to keep up with the girls, who were two paces ahead of him. They'd told him everything they'd heard as they'd run down the stairs.

"Maybe it'll be like the show, where the contestants sing in front of judges sitting on giant swings." Zaiba reached out her arms, miming being on an imaginary swing.

"And then when one of the judge likes the singing, they *flyyyyyyy* through the air and sprinkle confetti down on the contestant." Poppy jumped up and pretended to throw confetti on Ali's head.

"Lucky contestant," the girls boomed together like a *Swing Sing* judge. "You're through to the next round!" Then they burst into fits of laughter.

But Zaiba's detective brain hadn't stopped working. "I wonder why this is the only hotel in town taking bookings?" She was still pondering this when they reached the annexe. But before they could even reach the patio doors, they burst open.

"There you are!" Jessica said, sounding relieved.

She was standing with a huge plate of samosas, which she handed to Ali. Rookie mistake. Didn't she know Ali held the school record for eating the most samosas in under a minute? "I thought all your exploring would have made you hung—" She suddenly stopped speaking as she stared at Zaiba's dress, and the look on her face was enough to kill any appetite Zaiba might have had.

"What on *earth* happened to your new clothes?" Jessica's smile had disappeared. "Have you any idea how much they cost? Didn't your dad tell you to behave yourself?"

She grabbed a napkin from her purse and began to scrub at their dirty dresses. "There's no way you're going back to the party looking like this. Let's go clean you up."

"But we want to feed Sam the sweets and pastries. We can't miss it!" Zaiba protested.

"Then you'd better stop talking and start walking!"

Glumly, they all trooped back into the main building.

"Your dad will be so—" A muffled bark sliced through Jessica's words. Almost immediately there was the sound of claws scrabbling down the main stairwell and then a little furry head appeared round the corner. It was the pedigree pup!

Roberto's little legs scrambled on the shiny marble

stairs but nevertheless he came bounding towards them in the lobby. Ali quickly dropped the plate of samosas on the floor and lunged to grab Roberto, but his arms closed around thin air as the dog slipped past him, his tiny pink mouth plucking a samosa from the plate as he did. He bounded joyfully off one of the leather couches in the lobby and carried the stolen samosa out through the open door into the hotel drive, where he paused to gobble up the flaky pastry.

Jessica looked from Roberto to Zaiba and back again. "What ... who ... did a dog just steal one of our samosas?"

Before anyone could answer, a screech came from the top of the stairwell. "Oh my gosh! Roberto's escaped!" There was a blur of fur as the dog disappeared out of the main door.

Suddenly Maysoon's entourage was storming down the stairs, most of them in clothes that looked very fashionable but not at all suited to running.

Jessica blinked once, very carefully as though she didn't trust herself to do anything else. She took a long, juddering breath. "This doesn't have anything to do with your messy clothes, does it?"

Zaiba swallowed hard. What would Eden Lockett do right now? There was no way she could explain how important that pup was without admitting they'd gone too far in their mission to find out who the celebrity was, and spied on Maysoon. There was only one thing for it — go after the dog!

She grabbed Poppy and Ali's hands and dragged them out of the hotel's main entrance.

"Where are you going now?" Jessica called after them.

Zaiba paused at the open door. "To make everything better — you'll see! Trust me." She crossed her fingers behind her back, hoping her stepmum would have faith in them.

Jessica shook her head. "Trust you to do what? Oh ... go on then."

"Yes!" Ali punched the air and the three of them bounded out on to the drive, one after the other. "What is it we're going to do exactly?"

"Grab a greyhound, with any luck. Follow me!" said Zaiba.

There was a shout from the lobby behind them. Without breaking speed, they swerved round the side of the hotel and immediately spotted another crowd of people, this time all hotel staff, racing after a small glossy fast thing on four legs.

Mr Ainsley lunged for the pup but Roberto gracefully dived through his arms, as though the hotel manager was holding out an agility hoop for him to jump through. His little pink tongue lolled out the side of his mouth as he ran, scattering samosa crumbs.

"Catch that dog!" Mr Ainsley wailed. More and more people joined the chase, with Zaiba and her friends bringing up the rear. Roberto bounded into the fountain, splashing happily for a moment before heading towards the annexe, where the Mehndi party was still in full swing.

Zaiba felt a prickle travel down her arms as she saw a glimpse of the future. She dreaded what was going to happen next, but she guessed it would involve a dog, a Mehndi party and Sam. Sam, who was absolutely *terrified* of dogs.

"Someone get my baby!" she heard Maysoon cry, as she came round the corner. Her entourage flooded past her as she stood with her hands on her hips and stared out on to the drive. "Georgia, organize the search party! What do I hire you all for?"

By her side, Georgia the PA barked instructions.

"I think I saw him by the shrubbery!"

"We need him back! His pedicure is at six!"

"Was that a lamb samosa? He's vegetarian!"

But Zaiba knew that something much worse than Roberto breaking his diet was about to happen. If Sam even caught a glimpse of a dog's tail, she would be a wreck. And Zaiba had promised her cousin that she would make sure nothing bad happened at her party. She couldn't break her promise.

She *had* to catch that dog before something truly awful took place!

7
PUPPY PANDEMONIUM

Zaiba counted quickly as she watched a stream of people running towards the annexe. Five hotel staff, seven entourage members, the journalist and more photographers than she could count. All chasing after one little dog! The greyhound yapped and barked with delight, as though this was the best game ever.

"He's just getting more excited," Zaiba said. "We need to calm him down!"

But no one was listening to her as they continued to chase Roberto – straight towards the doors of the function hall.

"No!" yelled Zaiba. "Sam is afraid of dogs!"

"Did you know that's called cynophobia?" Ali panted as he struggled to keep up.

"Not now!" said Zaiba.

Roberto was already closing in on the doors to the function hall. Faster and faster, Zaiba and her friends raced between the crowd of people, but just then the patio door began to swing open – the door opening out on to the garden, which Zaiba had noticed earlier. Perfect for a dog to leap through.

"No, stop!" Zaiba cried, but it was too late. A large hand smattered with hair grasped the brass door handle and a face emerged – a face she recognized. Her dad!

"Ah, Zaiba, you'll never guess what Auntie Sabeen just— OH!"

Roberto threw himself against Zaiba's dad then dashed between his legs, throwing him off balance as he raced away.

"Woah!" Time seemed to slow down as Zaiba watched her dad topple, tremble, sway and lean, until with a crash he tumbled to the floor. Zaiba leaped over his body, quickly glancing down at his wide eyes and open mouth as Ali and Poppy did the same.

"Coming through!" cried Ali.

"No time to stop!" explained Poppy.

"Sorry, Dad! Puppy pandemonium!" Zaiba panted, racing ahead. *Where was Roberto?*

A horrified shriek came from the direction of the small stage. It was too late. Sam had caught sight of the greyhound and her whole body was trembling. Just as one of her aunties was about to feed her a sugary pastry, Sam jumped up on to the ornate sofa, her newly decorated hands waving frantically. Icing sugar flew everywhere, covering her sari in a fine white dusting.

"It that a *dog*? Someone get it out of here!" Sam cried.

Zaiba rushed over to her shrieking cousin, just missing Roberto who had joined her on the sofa and was trying to lick the henna on her feet before dashing off again. This time heading for the buffet table...

"Oh no you don't, you rascal!" Tanvir bellowed. He lunged for Roberto, who had hopped up on to the table, and missed, crashing into the table and sending plates of meat and salad flying.

"Roberto, no!" Zaiba and Poppy cried out in unison. But it was too late, the pup lost his balance on the wobbling table and stumbled straight on to the beautifully decorated cake that Hassan had made, leaving paw prints in the icing.

"Nooooooo!" Hassan cried, his arms reaching out in despair. The loud noise spooked Roberto, who stole another samosa and then fled out of the patio doors and back into the hotel grounds.

Sam burst into tears and sank down in a heap on the sofa. "Not our beautiful cake!" she wailed. Sadly, she looked down at her sticky sari and the spot on her feet that Roberto had licked. The henna design had become smudged and smeared, not having dried yet. Zaiba came over to comfort Sam and noticed that the SamTan design on her arm had also been destroyed.

"Maybe we could fix it..." she tried.

"No, no, it's gone. This was *supposed* to show how long our love would l-l-last!" Sam burst into tears again.

"My beautiful cake," Hassan howled. "It took me five hours!"

He walked over to his niece to put a comforting arm round her shoulder, though it seemed more like *he* was the one who needed support.

Zaiba rushed over to the patio doors and peered out into the garden. The fairy lights strung along the path revealed a trail of muddy footprints and some blue icing sugar on the white stone walkway. They seemed to lead over to the pond and then – Zaiba squinted harder – no. It was no use. The grounds were huge and she couldn't see any further. If only she had a pair of super-strong binoculars to capture his escape route.

"Mr Rollings, after that dog!" Mr Ainsley commanded, appearing through the crowd. Mr Rollings was the dutiful, if a little out-of-shape, doorman. Zaiba and the crowd watched as he jogged outside, only to return a few minutes later, red-faced and empty-handed.

"Not a whiff of him, sir. How did the dog even escape?"

"A chamber maid has reported that the next-door room had left their door open. He clambered over the balcony fence and straight out of their room."

Zaiba's stomach lurched. She was *sure* she had shut the door behind her. Or maybe she'd been in such a rush to get back to the party, she'd forgotten... She felt a firm hand land on her shoulder and looked up. It was her dad, his brow creased into a frown.

"Zaiba," he said in a quiet voice. "I want you to go back to the hotel room, now. I don't know how you were involved in this but you can explain later."

Zaiba started to say something but her dad's face grew even sterner. She nodded. She wanted more than *anything* to run into the grounds and search for Roberto, but now wasn't a good time.

"The same goes for you two." Her dad looked at Poppy and Ali, shaking his head. "I'm disappointed. If your father is flat out on the floor, you help him, you don't use him for hurdle practice! Respect your elders." He shook his head one final time and then pushed his way through the crowd back towards the sobbing Sam.

"I was quite proud of that jump," Ali whispered. "His tummy was really sticking up into the air!"

"Ali, don't," Poppy said, a pleading look on her face. "We're in enough trouble as it is. I hope he doesn't tell my mum." She looked at Zaiba. "What should we do now?"

Zaiba thought for a moment. "We lie low. Let's head back to the hotel room and regroup."

"You mean do as we're told?" Ali raised his eyebrows. "Radical."

The trio silently slipped past the partygoers, who had gathered in huddles and were whispering to each other. Snippets floated over, such as "naughty dog" and "spoilt" and "see those children?". It was all too much. Zaiba was sure Roberto wasn't really naughty, even if he was a bit spoilt. He just liked food, like most dogs!

As they approached the grand marble lobby, they saw the small press team that had been doing interviews earlier. They had gathered in a semicircle around Maysoon. Zaiba, Ali and Poppy wriggled their way to the front of the group as journalists fired questions at the celebrity.

"Can you confirm the dog's name?"

"Maysoon, are you aware that #dogdisaster is the number one trending topic online?"

"Did you let the dog out?"

Georgia was furiously scribbling on a clipboard, trying to keep a record of all the questions.

"Maysoon had *absolutely* nothing to do with this!" she boomed. Her pen flew into the air and landed by Poppy's feet.

Poppy picked up the pen for her and handed it back over. "Oh, a personalized pen!" Along the barrel was WH in gold lettering.

"Give me that!" Georgia snapped, snatching back the pen. "I mean ... thank you."

The journalist with the thick black eyebrows noticed and picked up on the tension.

"Excuse me. I'm Damon Harvey with VIPTV." He pushed a microphone into Georgia's face. "I've heard talk that this is just a publicity stunt to promote Maysoon's new film? Do you want to comment on that Ms...?"

"Ms Stevens," Georgia replied nervously. "And no. No, we do not!"

She quickly led Maysoon away from the prying journalists and into a private room.

"Oh, we need to plan a search party immediately!" Zaiba heard Maysoon sigh as she was led away. "I also need a camomile tea." She paused in the doorway and threw a pleading look back at the gathered journalists and photographers. "Someone, please! Loose leaf only!"

"What's loose leaf?" Ali asked as Georgia followed Maysoon. She gave one final glare at the group gathered in the lobby, before slamming the door shut.

Most of the assembled press team started milling about, drinking coffee and checking their phones. None of them seemed to care about finding Roberto, they just wanted Maysoon. It looked as though these investigative journalists weren't as good as their job titles. Zaiba felt a thrill of anticipation. *But I could investigate!* She felt her detective skills kicking in again. The mission to find a celebrity had been fun, but this was a real-life puzzle.

Zaiba heard soft footsteps behind her and turned round. A teary Sam had emerged from the Mehndi party. Zaiba felt her heart sink to her stomach at the sight of her cousin looking so devastated on her big day. But Sam's tears suddenly dried up as she watched a waitress scurry through Maysoon's door, carrying a tea tray. They just caught glimpse of the star, reaching for the silver teapot as a member of staff softly shut the door.

"Was that...?" she breathed, wide-eyed.

"Yep." Poppy smiled. "It's Maysoon!"

"Wow," Sam said shakily. "I'm her biggest fan! I'd give anything to meet her. Imagine if I could get a photo."

A light bulb suddenly pinged in Zaiba's mind. *That's it!* She hadn't been able to protect Sam from Roberto, but maybe she could make things right again.

"Darling." Tanvir appeared by Sam's side, doing his best to put on a brave smile. "We're about to cut the cake."

"The ruined cake? That the ... dog ... touched," Sam asked, her eyes filling with tears again.

"Well. Yes. But we've cut round the paw prints and honestly you can't tell the difference," Tanvir tried his best to cheer her up as he led her back to the party.

Zaiba turned back to Poppy and Ali. "I have to do something to make Sam's party special again. Something to clear this mess up," she said, chewing her lip.

"Don't you think you've done enough already?" a voice said from the main doorway. Mariam was standing there, her arms folded.

"Leave us alone, Mariam," Ali replied.

"Everyone's talking about how Sam's Mehndi party will be remembered – a doggy disaster. I don't know what you did, Zaiba," Mariam said. "But I'm sure you three are behind this chaos." Her eyes narrowed.

She shook her head in disgust then turned and walked back towards the function hall, closing the doors behind her. Zaiba watched her cousin leave. Why was Mariam always turning up at the worst moments? Why couldn't she just leave Zaiba alone?

"Come on, let's go." With a sigh, she turned to lead the others to their room, but just then there was a sound from Mr Ainsley's office.

"This is a disaster!" Mr Ainsley came out of his office to stand behind the reception desk. If he'd had any hair left, he'd have been tearing it out. "I knew getting to host Maysoon's champagne reception so last minute was too good to be true!"

"But you were so excited about it..." Liza ventured timidly.

"Of course I was!" Mr Ainsley paced up and down behind the desk. "But that's only because we got to host it instead of that blasted White Hall with their all-glass solar-powered ceiling and their self-check-in machine!"

"Ah yes... Why couldn't they host Maysoon?" Liza asked.

Mr Ainsley's eyes glinted, or perhaps they just caught the light of his extremely shimmering cufflinks. "Their self-check-in machine had an ... unfortunate meltdown and ended up switching the names around. They had to cancel all their bookings. But that would never happen with our good old-fashioned *human* receptionist, would it?"

Liza nodded, keeping her eyes firmly fixed to the ground.

"Wow," Poppy whispered. "Mr Ainsley seems like a tough boss..."

"Or just a meanie," Ali suggested.

"Now, where are we with the search party for the runaway dog?" Mr Ainsley barked, not unlike a dog himself.

As the staff began scurrying in all directions, Zaiba noticed something sticking out of the back of the rubbish bin on the far side of the lobby. She hurried over and tugged on the loose end that was poking out of the bottom of the bin. It seemed like a long piece of rope but made of leather... She tugged and tugged and out flew—

"Roberto's lead!" she announced, holding the lead aloft.

"Where did you find that?" Mr Ainsley snapped, grabbing the lead.

"Be careful, Mr Ainsley, we don't want to contaminate the evidence," she said seriously.

"Evidence? But it's just a lead!" Mr Ainsley cried, carefully holding the lead between his thumb and forefinger.

"The lead was found in the bin." Zaiba raised her voice so that the assembled staff could hear her. "I have reason to believe that it was deliberately taken off Roberto and disposed of here. Roberto didn't escape he was—"

"Kidnapped!" Liza suggested, looking excited by the potential mystery.

"Maybe not kidnapped," Zaiba quickly added. "But encouraged to run off, perhaps." She decided not to mention that it might have been *her* who had forgotten to close the door that allowed Roberto to run away.

Mr Ainsley, who had been staring at the lead, seemed to snap out of his daze. "Right, thank you. But now I think it's time you went on your way. Off you go."

Zaiba, Poppy and Ali were reluctantly making their way up the stairs when Maysoon swung open the door of her private lounge and strode into the lobby.

Her face crumpled at the sight of Roberto's lead but

no Roberto and she began sobbing, silently this time, her shoulders shaking. It was almost too much for Zaiba to bear.

Before they went any further, the trio looked back at the scene. Maysoon scanned the group in the lobby. She straightened her shoulders and looked from face to face. "I just have one question for you all. *Who let Roberto off his lead?*"

8
ZAIBA GOES CLIMBING

Thud... Thud... Thud...

Thud... Thud... Thud...

Thud—

"Ali, cut that out!" Zaiba snapped. "The other guests will complain!"

Ali paused from where he'd been repeatedly (and annoyingly) throwing a rubber ball against the wall of Poppy and Zaiba's room. He'd already tried to keep himself occupied with ten sudoku puzzles but that had only taken him twenty minutes. No one in their family completed sudoku faster than Ali.

Zaiba took a deep breath. She had been on edge with

nervous excitement after hearing Maysoon's words just after they had been ushered out of the lobby. "*Who let Roberto off his lead?*"

As if reading her mind, Poppy asked a question in a shaky voice. "Do you think we should tell the grown-ups what you saw? The hands letting Roberto off his lead?"

THUD.

"Are you mad?" Ali almost screeched, finally stopping his game with the rubber ball. "That would mean telling them we were snooping on the celebrity *and* that we went up into the attic—"

"She's only trying to help," Zaiba said in a soft voice.

The three of them fell into silence, their brows furrowed and arms crossed. There was a crime unfolding before them and they needed a place to begin their investigations.

"Come on." Zaiba perked up. She was the head agent and it was her duty to keep her team in high spirits. "Why don't we sit out on the balcony? We'll go crazy squashed up in here."

They settled themselves in the lawn chairs on their

balcony, breathing in the dusk air and gazing out over the glittering lights of the town. Far below, the sound of a gentle melody floated up on the breeze. Zaiba chewed her lip. She had promised Sam that her Mehndi party would be disaster free, and yet a dog on the loose had managed to spoil everything. This wasn't what she'd wanted for her cousin at all. Zaiba shook her head. Then she had an idea. If she found Roberto for Maysoon, maybe then the singer would agree to meet Sam. And surely that would save her ruined party?

"This hotel has a *biiiiiggg* garden," Poppy said, interrupting her thoughts.

"It's 2.5 acres," Ali informed her. "Not including the maze."

"There's a maze?" Poppy asked. "Where?"

Zaiba snapped back into detective mode and pulled the map from the back of her book. She pointed to the maze. "It's in the north-eastern corner of the grounds. I drew this little compass by the side so we can check the direction against it."

She looked up into the evening sky, her eyes searching

for the brightest star in the sky – the North Star! She spotted it floating above the tennis courts at the far end of the grounds. Then she remembered the sentence they were taught at school – *naughty elephants squirt water* to show the order of north, east, south and west. Using her arm like a compass she turned to east and tracked down until...

"There! I see it!" She pointed towards a group of hedges arranged in a geometric pattern.

As Poppy and Ali stared in the direction that Zaiba had pointed, Zaiba hurriedly got out *Eden Lockett's Detective Handbook* and flipped through it. Using the light flooding out of the room behind them, she was able to find the page she wanted. Aha! She stabbed a finger at a little diagram.

"I knew it," she said. "There's a maze in *Eden Lockett's Detective Handbook*. It's a bird's-eye view diagram."

"What's that?" Poppy asked.

"A drawing of how the maze would look from above," Ali said, always eager to share his knowledge.

"No, I mean what's that?" Poppy pointed to a scribble

in the margin of the book and looked at Zaiba.

"Oh..." Zaiba hesitated. "That's a note from my mum."

Ali patted his sister on the arm and went back into the bedroom to give them some space. He wasn't a big fan of any talk that involved emotions.

"You mean your stepmum, Jessica?" Poppy asked.

Zaiba took a breath. "No, my birth mum. She was called Nabiha but I call her Ammi." Zaiba explained tentatively. She had never told her best friend all the details before, but now that Poppy had met her *entire* family it seemed right.

"My dad doesn't really talk about it, but based on what he's told me and Aunt Fouzia sharing some stories... I think she was in another country when she passed away."

"Oh no. I'm sorry, Zaiba."

"It's OK, I was very young so I don't really remember. And Dad is happy now that he's met Jessica."

"I like Jessica a lot. She lets me borrow her lip gloss!"

The girls giggled.

"I got my Eden Lockett books from Ammi." Zaiba's voice softened as she turned the battered old novel over in her hands. The cover was dog-eared from constant handling, over the years. "The perfect reminder of my real mum. They first came out when Ammi and Aunt Fouzia were little. These are first editions!"

"Ohhhhhhh," Poppy said. "So *that* explains it."

"Explains what?" Was Poppy turning her detective skills on Zaiba?

"Why you're so determined to be an agent. It's not just because of Aunt Fouzia. Your mum was obsessed too!"

Zaiba laughed. "I suppose Ammi is a bit of a mystery to me..."

"Zaiba," Poppy said, pulling her friend into a hug, "Thanks for telling me about your ammi."

"Now we can read the notes together!" Zaiba smiled. They both began to study the words in the margin:

What's the difference between a maze and a labyrinth?

Maze = multicursal

Labyrinth = unicursal

Hmmm. Maybe solving a crime is like walking in a maze!

"Ummmm, what on *earth* does that mean?" Poppy said, frowning.

"I have no idea," admitted Zaiba. "But my ammi was definitely clever..."

Ali must have been listening from inside because he came running out on to the balcony to take the book from Zaiba and study the pages.

Poppy laughed. "I thought you weren't interested in our little chat?" She winked at Zaiba.

Ali ignored her, staring so hard at the diagram that his nose nearly touched the page. Suddenly, he spun the book round and pointed at the maze.

"It means that with a maze you have options, but with a labyrinth there's only one correct route." He smiled triumphantly.

Zaiba patted her brother proudly on the head as she stared at the maze in the distance. When it came to solving the mystery of who let Roberto off his lead and why, what were their options? Ammi's words were starting to make complete sense – it did feel as though they were in a maze!

"So who are our prime suspects, agents? We know it has to be someone who was in the room with Roberto during that press conference. I'm sure we can figure this out together!"

Ali suddenly shot upright. "Hey, I have a theory! What if it was just a mistake? One of the hotel staff let him off the lead and then threw away the lead when they realized what they'd done?"

"The staff seem to be afraid of Mr Ainsley," Poppy agreed. "It would make sense that they're too afraid to own up."

Zaiba nodded slowly. "It's a good theory, but I think it was done on purpose... We'll need evidence before we can accuse anyone. What about the journalist, Damon? He was in the room during the interview *and* he seemed weirdly excited when he accused Maysoon of setting the whole thing up."

"Also, I don't trust anyone with eyebrows *that* dramatic." Poppy wiggled her own eyebrows around in imitation.

Zaiba giggled and gazed out at the distant hedges

of the maze. Out of the corner of her eye she saw a flash of something and her thoughts suddenly snapped into focus.

"Oh. My. Word," she breathed.

She was *certain* she'd just seen a flash of grey near the centre of the maze. A flash of grey that could only be—

"Roberto!" Poppy shouted as she leaped up.

"Right." Zaiba's eyes narrowed as she felt an excited shiver pass over her. "We *have* to get that dog." Hopefully that would make everything better for Sam and Maysoon. Then they'd try to uncover who had let Roberto off his lead. No dog should be allowed to roam around like that. It was totally irresponsible *and* he didn't have his tweed jacket on. He might catch a cold!

"But what if someone comes looking for us?" Ali said.

"Let's not worry about that now. Look, if we can catch Roberto, Maysoon will be happy again, and maybe she'll agree to meet Sam and we can make *her* happy again, and then Dad won't be angry with us and EVERYONE will be happy again!" Zaiba stopped for breath.

Ali and Poppy stared at her in shock.

"OK, I think we need to get that dog." Poppy nodded.

"Or Zaiba might explode..." Ali muttered under his breath.

Zaiba stared at the door to their room. How would they get out unseen? She went over to it and peered out into the corridor. Two hotel porters were walking up and down the corridor, apparently on "high-alert" for any doggy sightings. There was no way the three of them could get past those porters without being spotted. She snuck back into the room and quietly shut the door behind her. She leaned her forehead against the polished wood, thinking. *What would Aunt Fouzia do in a situation like this?*

Ali whistled from where he was leaning over the balcony. "Zaiba, come here! I think I have an idea."

He pointed at a wooden trellis, nailed to the hotel wall. "Each rung of this trellis is nine point six inches long. I know because I always carry a ruler with me." He tapped his back pocket.

"Who carries a ruler around with them?" Poppy laughed.

"As I was saying," Ali continued, ignoring her. "There are ten rungs of trellis to climb down each floor of the hotel and twelve inches in a foot, meaning each floor is eight-foot tall. We're two floors up so it's a sixteen-foot drop to the ground. We're all between four and five feet, so that means it's only just four times our body height to climb down."

Zaiba was silent for a moment and she felt like the cogs in her brain were whizzing around in overdrive. "Are you saying we could do it?"

Ali smiled. "I'm saying we could definitely do it."

Luckily it was quiet in the grounds below their balcony, so they should be able to climb down without being spotted.

Eden Lockett's golden rule number five popped into Zabia's head again: *A good agent always ensures the safety of her friends.* Zaiba took her time as she inspected the trellis, which was lit up by chandeliers burning bright inside the hotel. It was securely fastened to the wall – good. There were multiple handholds and places to balance their feet – perfect for climbing. They were only two floors up. If the worst came to the worst there was soft lawn below and a huge hydrangea bush to break their fall. If they fell... Zaiba winced. It was worth a shot.

"All right," she said. "Let's do it. Good thinking, Ali." Her little brother pulled his shoulders back and grinned with pride.

"Who'll go first?" Poppy said, peering down at the lawn uncertainly.

Thinking of Eden Lockett's fifth golden rule again, Zaiba bravely volunteered to lead the way. She perched on the wide balcony railing to find her balance. Then she reached out a foot to the trellis and tested it with her weight. It was nice and steady. She reached out a hand, then the other, then her other foot and ... she was climbing! Slowly but surely she made her way down, even passing by Aunt Fouzia's window on the way. Aunt Fouzia had requested a room on the ground floor because she found it difficult to walk up stairs after her famous case of 1986. It had involved an international football player, an attempt to steal antique jewellery and a life-or-death chase through the National Museum of Pakistan!

Zaiba froze for a second as she saw her auntie's outline through the net curtain, but she had her back to the window and was busy looking in a mirror. *What's she doing in her room?* Zaiba wondered. *She must have gone to freshen up... Don't turn round, don't turn round!* Zaiba wished silently. After a moment, her aunt wandered into the bathroom, humming to herself. Phew! Onwards Zaiba went, or rather downwards, leaping safely on to the lawn. She craned her head back and circled a hand through the air, beckoning Poppy down after her.

She watched her best friend, who had changed into leggings, make her way down. Poppy kept her eyes fixed firmly on the wall in front of her, clearly terrified even though she was now only eight feet above the ground. She moved ever so slowly and Zaiba began to wonder if Poppy would ever make it. But finally her best friend jumped softly to the ground beside her. Zaiba cheered and gave her a high five – Poppy had shown the bravery of a true agent.

Immediately Ali nimbly climbed down the trellis, moving like Spider-Man down the wall, descending much more quickly than either Zaiba or Poppy. Zaiba felt a twinge of jealousy. "I wish I was that fast," she muttered to Poppy. Ali jumped the last bit, before straightening up and coolly brushing down his shirt.

"That was so quick, Ali! A very useful detective skill. You're really coming on," Zaiba praised Ali. "Now let's hurry. There's no time to lose."

She turned towards the maze at the far end of the garden. The three of them ran over the manicured lawns, avoiding the lit garden paths where they might be seen, until they made it to the entrance of the maze.

Zaiba glanced over at the function hall. She could see figures moving about in the patio windows, bobbing and swaying as they danced. Up on the stage she could just make out Sam sitting miserably with Tanvir holding her hand. Zaiba's fists clenched in determination — she had to make her cousin smile again.

She glanced up at the hotel. A window shone like a beacon with a shining chandelier hanging from the ceiling – it was Maysoon's suite. A solitary figure stood silhouetted at the window, gazing down over the garden.

"We'll get your doggie for you, don't worry!" Zaiba whispered into the air.

"Are you talking to yourself?" Ali asked. "You know that's the first sign of—"

"Genius!" Poppy slapped her hand across Ali's mouth and pulled him to her, tussling his hair. "Stop teasing your sister!" He wriggled and groaned until she let him go, then he stood up, pushing the hair out of his eyes.

"What now?" he asked, peering into the first path of the maze. Luckily the hotel had also laced the hedges of the maze with fairy lights, lighting the path for them in an array of dancing colours.

"Now," Zaiba said. "We find Roberto." Above the music from the hotel, they heard a small yip. "He's definitely in there. This way, come on!"

9
FOLLOW THAT DOG!

Zaiba raced forwards, leading Poppy and Ali beneath an arch of leaves that marked the entrance to the maze. As they plunged inside, the hedges that had seemed so small from the balcony suddenly towered all around them.

Zaiba stumbled to a halt to make another voice recording. "We have entered the hotel maze, visibility is poor, we are short for time ... but I'm sure we'll find Roberto soon," she said, smiling as hopefully as she could at her team.

"Yeah, maybe if we were giants," Ali said, reaching up on tiptoe, trying to peer over one of the hedges. No hope – it was twice as tall as him.

Zaiba was getting frustrated. She turned off her phone. "Come on. From the balcony it looked like Roberto was in the centre of the maze. We can't give up at the first hurdle." Zaiba marched round the first bend of the maze. But as they turned the corner, the path immediately forked in two directions! She glanced around for any sign of a tiny dog, but ... nothing.

"What about the second hurdle?" Ali groaned.

Poppy's head bobbed as she looked between the two paths. "Which should we take? It's so confusing!"

"It's meant to be confusing," Zaiba replied. "It's a maze! Remember that Eden Lockett mystery – I think it was number eight."

Poppy's eyes lit up. "It was number seven – *The Mystery of Grey Gardens*! Eden tracked down..." She bit her lip, thinking hard. "A ghost in a maze!"

"That's right. And how did she do it?" Zaiba asked. The two friends often tested each other on Lockett facts. It was a good way to help them become the best agents they could be.

"It's in chapter five," Zaiba gently prompted her best

friend. "When Eden found the centre of the maze by keeping her left hand on the hedge ..."

"... and only taking left turns!" Poppy's face lit up.

"But—" Ali started to say something, when an excited *yip!* came from the heart of the maze.

"Shh, Ali. Roberto's in there! We need to get going!" Zaiba cut him off.

"Fine. We'll try it *your* way," Ali muttered.

Zaiba ignored him and reached out her left hand, following the path to their left. Poppy copied Zaiba and set off after her, giving Ali a stern look to follow.

"Why does no one ever listen to me?" Zaiba heard her brother whisper.

The three of them traced their fingertips over the left hedge, the bright green leaves releasing a sweet scent. They walked round and round, taking a left at each bend in the path. Luckily the small lanterns that lit the maze were still on, so they could make out their shadowy surroundings.

"If we weren't in the middle of a doggy disaster, this could be fun," Poppy said, revelling in the excitement of a

maze in the dark. The sound of the wedding party drifted over from the function room's open patio doors. Beyond that, Zaiba felt certain she could hear the quiet sobbing of a celebrity whose dog was missing.

"We have to stay focused, Poppy," Zaiba reminded her friend. "This could be life or death!"

"Whose death?" Ali grumbled.

"Shush, Ali!" Poppy and Zaiba said in unison. Then Zaiba felt bad – Ali was only trying to help. She put a hand in her pocket and passed him a sticky laddu that she had cleverly wrapped in yellow paper. "Here, we need to keep our energy up."

They kept going left, left and left again. Eventually, Zaiba broke out into a run as she heard a yowl of despair from further into the maze. But so many twists and turns were starting to make her feel dizzy, and then ... *wait*.

"Am I seeing double or does this all look a bit familiar?" she asked, stumbling to a halt.

"Of course it looks familiar!" Ali cried through a mouthful of laddu. "We're back where we started."

Zaiba looked around frantically. He was right!

They were at the entrance to the maze – again. She kicked a pile of leaves in frustration. They had wasted time and Roberto might run off at any second.

"I tried to tell you," Ali said.

From somewhere in the distance they heard a muffled bark. Roberto! He must have sensed people nearby and wanted to play.

"All right, Mr Smarty-pants," Zaiba grumbled, pacing up and down the path. "We should have listened. So, why didn't it work?"

Ali grinned. He picked up a twig and began sketching a rough outline of the maze in the dirt. "Because this isn't a maze ... it's a labyrinth."

Poppy and Zaiba shared an impressed glance. Zaiba really should listen to her brother more often.

"I noticed from the balcony, and with the note your ammi wrote in the margin, it just made sense," Ali explained. "With a labyrinth it isn't about left or right. It's about working out which is the *one* path that leads to the centre."

"And how do we do that?" asked Poppy.

"Every time we reach a dead end, we need to make a mark," said Ali, as Zaiba and Poppy watched him draw diagrams in the dirt. "Eventually there will be only one path without a mark on it – the path that leads to Roberto!" An excited *yip* rang out from a little dog who had just heard his name.

"Wow!" Poppy exclaimed. "I'm impressed, Ali."

"Good work!" Zaiba beamed. She spotted a pile of short bamboo canes bundled at the maze's entrance. The hotel gardener must have left them there for the evening. "We can use these to mark the paths that have dead ends."

They each grabbed a handful of canes and hastily set off, following one path after the other. They worked quickly – each time they hit a dead end, they left a couple of sticks in a "X" and quickly ran back to make their way to the next path.

Eventually there was only one path left.

"This must be it!" Zaiba cried breathlessly.

They grabbed each other's hands and ran down the winding path towards the sound of a snuffling nose, until finally...

"Roberto!" all three of them cheered at the same time.

The little Italian greyhound jumped up from where he'd being lying and ran over to them, his tail wagging so hard that it looked like a blur of grey fur. He jumped up and scrambled at their legs until Zaiba scooped him up in a big hug. His whole body was trembling with excitement and he arched his head to give Zaiba a big lick on the cheek.

"Well, Roberto, have you finished your tour of the hotel grounds?" Ali said.

"Wait," Zaiba gasped as she stroked Roberto's neck. "His collar. It's gone!"

"You mean the diamond collar?" Poppy's eyes grew wide.

Zaiba clicked her fingers. "Of course. It wasn't Roberto someone was trying to steal, it was his bling!"

Out of the corner of her eye, Zaiba noticed Ali crouching down by the birdbath that marked the centre of the maze.

"Uh, Zaiba..." He cocked his head to one side. "Do fancy hotels usually leave plates of grilled steak and sausages out in the grounds?"

Zaiba carefully put Roberto down and ran over to where Ali was standing and sure enough, there on the floor was a large dinner plate adorned with a prime steak and a string of juicy sausages! There were bite marks and chunks taken out of the meat and Zaiba saw Roberto licking his lips.

"I suppose you aren't vegetarian by *choice*," Poppy muttered, stroking the dog's head.

Zaiba leaned back on her feet, staring up at Poppy and Ali. "You know what this means, don't you?"

"Roberto came out here for a secret meat feast?" Ali suggested.

Zaiba nodded. "Sort of. Someone intended to lure Roberto here. When we left the balcony door open, we accidently helped them. Once he had escaped, it could have taken him a while to make it here but they must have known that eventually the smell of the meat would draw him out. Then they could steal his collar! The Mehndi party was a distraction but their plan worked."

"Poor Roberto." Poppy cuddled the pup who looked

exhausted from all the excitement and his big meal. "He probably hadn't had meat in so long that the smell was irresistible, even from so far away!"

Zaiba started taking pictures of the crime scene with her phone. "We have to leave it exactly as it is so the police can eventually search the area properly. But I've got these snaps just in case it gets disturbed."

She looked up at the dark sky and took a deep breath, her head spinning. "First we went on our mission to find out the identity of a mystery celebrity."

"Tick!" Poppy excitedly drew an invisible tick in the air with a finger.

"Then we began our search for a missing dog!"

"TICK!" Poppy drew another, even bigger invisible tick in the air. Ali was looking at the two of them as though they had eaten way too much sugar. He knelt down to hold Roberto and stop him from trembling.

Zaiba gazed down at her brother and the dog. "And now we have to find out who let him off the lead and has taken the diamond collar." She could feel her own eyes growing as big as saucers. "Team, this is officially a full-blown detective case! We've gone from mission, to hunt, to investigation!"

Ali gazed into the dog's eyes. "Can you tell us who stole your collar, little guy?" Roberto gave a small whine and Ali ruffled his fur. "Thought not." He got to his feet. "So what do we do now, oh great detective?"

Zaiba started to think. "OK, let's stay calm. First things first, we need to get Roberto back to Maysoon, diamond collar or not."

"Agreed." Poppy nodded.

Zaiba hastily made a voice recording. "Subject secured, we will now head back to the celebrity's room."

She went to pick up Roberto but he darted from her grip – he thought this was another fun game. Zaiba made another grasp for him but this time he wriggled free and started running around in circles, chasing his tail.

"Did you say subject *secured*?" Ali giggled.

"He's not going to let me carry him," Zaiba grumbled. But how were they going to get Roberto out of the maze without his lead? "I suppose we're going to need some sort of…" Her glance settled on Ali's leather belt, "makeshift device."

She smiled sweetly at Ali and held out her hand. He threw Poppy a panicked glance but Poppy had her arms folded. Ali wasn't going to have any backup on this one.

"My belt? Really? Can't we just try and get him to follow us?" he begged.

Both Poppy and Zaiba shook their heads. Reluctantly, Ali undid his belt and handed it to his sister who wrapped it around Roberto's neck loosely, being careful not to hurt him. "There!"

Poppy couldn't help laughing. "It's not exactly the designer labels he's used to," she said.

Ali looked miserable. He clutched the waistband of his trousers in one fist to stop them from falling down. Jessica had bought the suit online especially for the party – but she had got it one size too big so he could wear it to cousin Anwar's wedding next summer as well.

He looked down at his trousers. "How do you expect

me to walk like this?"

Zaiba placed a reassuring hand on his arm. "You're rescuing a little Italian greyhound. You're a hero."

"Yes, I'm sure Superman *always* has his trousers around his ankles when he saves the day," Ali said, rolling his eyes.

"Come on then. Let's get you back to your mummy," Poppy cooed, stroking Roberto's head. He licked her hand in agreement and Zaiba led the way, retracing their steps through the maze.

"Do you think we'll get to meet Maysoon properly now?" Poppy said, her eyes sparkling.

"She's going to be over the moon!" breathed Zaiba. "She'll probably ask us to be her personal bodyguards for the rest of her stay here. We'd be better than the useless ones Mr Ainsley has stationed outside her room..."

Usually Poppy was the daydreamer, but Zaiba let herself imagine how cool it would be to be part of Maysoon's entourage. Maybe the three of them would even be given black suits with the walkie-talkie earpieces!

A few metres down the path, she glanced round and had to quickly stifle a giggle. Ali was bringing up the rear, trousers sagging as he tried to keep up with them.

"What was it the mummy tomato said to the baby tomato? Ketchup!" she joked.

"Don't," Ali grumbled, hitching up his trousers and trudging after them.

Finally, the entrance to the maze was in sight.

"Look!" Poppy pointed towards the leafy arch. "We made it!"

The large white shape of the hotel reared up and Zaiba felt a sudden movement on the end of the lead. "Roberto, no!" But it was too late. The greyhound had slipped his head out of the belt's loop and darted off across the gardens.

"Come back!" Poppy cried as the pooch bounded out of sight. "Where's he gone now?"

Zaiba ran out of the maze. Across the lawn, she spotted a set of tiny footprints in the earth around the flower beds, heading towards stone steps that led down to a doorway with the words *Cellar – STAFF ONLY* written on a wooden sign. She just caught sight of a tiny grey tail disappearing behind the open door.

"There." She pointed. "Follow that dog!"

10
STINKING BISHOP OR OLD SOCKS?

In the entrance of the dingy cellar Zaiba, Poppy and Ali huddled together, peering into the darkness.

"We need to be really quiet," Zaiba whispered to the others. "If Roberto hears us coming, he might bolt again."

"First the attic and now a creepy cellar," Ali said in a low voice. "Why do we keep going where spiders live?"

Zaiba felt sorry for her brother but being a detective meant exploring all sorts of unusual places.

She put her finger to her lips as they stepped inside. The cellar was dimly lit by a single flickering bulb, but she could make out large dusty shelves filled with bottles of expensive wine and round yellow cheeses. A stack of chairs covered in cobwebs balanced haphazardly in the corner, ready to topple over at any moment. This was definitely the dumping ground of the hotel!

"It smells like old P.E. socks down here," Poppy whispered, screwing up her nose in disgust.

"You're right," Zaiba whispered back. "But someone likes the smells down here."

Poppy followed Zaiba's gaze and saw Roberto. He was snuffling around the base of some wooden barrels, sending tiny spiders scuttling in every direction. Ali shuddered.

"It's OK," Zaiba reassured him. "They're money spiders – they bring good luck!"

Ali looked slightly less scared. "We need it."

Zaiba was determined to stay positive. She wouldn't give up – especially now that the mystery of a missing diamond collar was waiting to be solved. "Follow me and stay low. No sudden movements or Roberto will run." The little greyhound was so focused on the scent, maybe he wouldn't notice them approaching.

One step, two steps, three steps... Zaiba trod on the

balls of her feet to prevent any noise. Aunt Fouzia had taught her how to move silently across a room and it was paying off. Her plan had worked! Roberto didn't spot them until Zaiba had squeezed behind the barrels and was bending over him. He looked up happily as she slipped the belt over his head, on a tighter notch this time.

"Those puppy-dog eyes won't work on me," Zaiba whispered. "You shouldn't have run off, you naughty pooch!" But she didn't have the heart to really tell him off – he was so adorable!

She gave him a little pat on the head then straightened up. Now they could finally get this pup back to Maysoon. Zaiba began to step out from behind the barrels, when—

"What are *you* doing down here?" came a deep voice from the other side of the shelves.

The three of them froze and Zaiba's heart began thumping loudly in her chest. They'd been found out! But before she could compose a reply, another voice rang out.

"Sorry, sir. I was just checking the temperature of the champagne for Maysoon's reception tomorrow."

Zaiba, Poppy and Ali slunk back behind the barrels. Zaiba peeped through a crack between the shelves and could just make out the hotel manager. Mr Ainsley was talking to the waiter with floppy hair. He'd been serving them at the Mehndi party *and* helping out in Maysoon's suite. Mr Ainsley sure worked his staff hard!

Roberto began to whine and pull on the lead, keen to meet these new playmates. Oh no! They'd be in so much trouble if anyone knew they were down here. She bugged her eyes at the others. *What are we going to do?*

Poppy scrabbled in her pocket and pulled out a samosa, then silently bent down to feed the treat to Roberto. He nibbled at the pastry, licking her fingers. That would keep him quiet for a while. Zaiba shot her friend a grateful look. *The sooner we get out of here the better.*

"I thought I told you to report to the kitchen and polish the glassware?" Mr Ainsley was saying. "Head up there now, please."

Zaiba peered further out to see if Mr Ainsley looked as annoyed as he sounded.

Aha! From this angle, Zaiba could just make out the

waiter's name badge, although it was difficult to read as his too-big shirt nearly hid it. Curly gold lettering spelled out the name: *Clark*. Zaiba shot a look at Poppy who nodded when she saw the badge.

Her hands itched to make a voice recording of her observations but she knew she'd be heard. *Wait!* A thought popped into her head. Eden Lockett's golden rule number two: *All good detectives make notes.* Zaiba pulled out *Eden Lockett's Detective Handbook* and began to scribble notes in the back. She wasn't going to miss a single clue!

"Yes, but, but ... the champagne!" Clark stammered, backing towards the crates. Poppy scooped up Roberto and they shrank against the damp wall. She hid Roberto's nose in the crook of her arm – the last thing she needed was another whine from the greyhound.

Zaiba watched Clark intently, hardly daring to breathe. She glanced over at Ali who had bundled himself into a tight ball with his eyes screwed shut. Zaiba felt a wave of sympathy for her brother before she turned to focus on the scene in front her. The waiter's eyes darted back and forth across the barrels until he set his lips in a firm line, as though deciding something. Then he threw himself forwards, crashing into the largest wooden barrel, which knocked over a nearby shelf of round cheeses that rolled and bounced across the sloping floor. Ali's eyes flew open in panic to see what the ruckus was.

"The Stinking Bishop cheese from Pierre's Delicatessen," Mr Ainsley gasped.

"I'm sorry," Clark said. Though Zaiba noticed he didn't look sorry at all. "I ... I tripped over a wine cork."

"He's lying," Poppy whispered, her eyes glittering with outrage.

"I know." Zaiba held a finger to her lips. They could share their observations later. Zaiba silently pressed "record" on her phone so she could listen back later for any clues.

Mr Ainsley was too flustered to notice Clark's thin smile. He flung himself across the cellar, chasing after a wheel of cheese as it rolled towards ... the shelves where they were hiding!

Zaiba grabbed the others and dragged them further down the aisle. Roberto started to wriggle and wag his tail wildly. *He's going to run!* she thought. Luckily Ali saw what was happening and started pulling funny faces at Roberto to distract him. Zaiba reminded herself to give her little bro a pat on the back when they got out of this squeeze. Once again, Zaiba's heart was beating so fast she was sure it would pop out of her chest. Would they be thrown out of the hotel? That scandal didn't bear thinking about – their mum and dad would never forgive them for embarrassing their family. They just needed to sneak out with Roberto, undetected.

Mr Ainsley caught the wheel of cheese just as it rolled to a halt before the shelves. He straightened up, lifting the cheese through the air as though it was a giant diamond on a velvet pillow. He went to place it back on the muslin square where all the other cheeses sat. Then he pulled a crisp linen handkerchief from his pocket and carefully wiped his hands clean. He took a deep breath, turning to Clark as a vein pulsed angrily on his forehead.

Mr Ainsley spoke carefully, clearly trying to stay

patient. "I know you're new here, Mr Stevens, but *please*. Stop. Messing. Things. Up. Honestly, between you and that useless receptionist, I don't know how I cope!" His voice went higher and higher until he was almost squeaking and his face turned beetroot-red. As he dropped his head in his hands, Clark's shoulders shook with repressed laughter.

"And I thought *I* had a strange sense of humour..." Ali whispered.

Zaiba frowned. For someone who was in the middle of being told off, Clark seemed very pleased with himself. He'd knocked over those cheeses on purpose, but why? Perhaps he just really disliked his boss... Zaiba could hardly blame him. Mr Ainsley had been rude to Liza and now this waiter, and all for what? Because he was super anxious about having a celebrity guest? That didn't seem fair. Or was Mr Ainsley always like this?

Clark cleared his throat. "Sir? Is there anything I can do to help?"

"I'm aware that I can be a perfectionist," Mr Ainsley said with a juddering breath. "We appreciate you stepping in to work these extra events so last minute. But you must be aware that I – I mean the hotel – is under *a lot* of pressure at the moment."

"So he's not a permanent waiter here," Zaiba whispered to herself.

"That explains why his uniform is more shabby and less chic than the others," Poppy added.

Zaiba nodded and gestured back to Mr Ainsley. He was instructing Clark to pick up the rest of the wheels of cheese. The waiter scrambled to place them all neatly back on the shelf, using the corner of a napkin to wipe stray bits of dust from the rinds.

"First, the King's Inn Hotel gets a bed bug infestation, then the Hill Hotel's pipes burst... Now the White Hall's ridiculous self-check-in machine has gone haywire. Where do you think all those guests are going to stay now?" Mr Ainsley continued, pacing up and down in the rather cramped space.

"I thought you'd be happy for the extra business?" Clark said coolly.

"Not when it has come from a string of *bad luck*!"

Zaiba saw a shiver run down Mr Ainsley's spine. "And this is an old hotel, we're not used to such a high demand, especially with these big events as well. We have lots of restoration work to do, though, which costs money. A lot of money. So at least the extra guests help with that."

Zaiba began inching closer and closer, still listening to the conversation. She didn't want to miss out on any potentially important clues!

"With a good restoration job, a celebrity endorsement *and* some good luck." Mr Ainsley's eyes glittered. "Perhaps we'll *finally* receive the four gold stars I've worked so hard for my entire career."

Clark nodded in agreement.

"Guess how many hotels in this town have four gold stars, Clark," Mr Ainsley said.

"Oh, I wouldn't know..." Clark murmured, replacing a wheel of cheese on a shelf.

"No, go on, guess!"

Clark screwed up his face in thought. "Um, none?"

"That's right!" Mr Ainsley said. "Not even the Summerway Hotel. Can you believe it? I thought for certain they would..."

Zaiba raised her eyebrows, Mr Ainsley *really* wanted those gold stars. And the smell of cheese was *really* making her nose itch. Zaiba pinched her nostrils together and tried not to let out the monstrous sneeze that was brewing.

Mr Ainsley gave Clark a firm slap on the back. "Finish up here and try not to ruin anything else, especially now you understand why everything has to be perfect." He made his way back up to the ground floor. "Then you can go and polish the glassware."

Clark waited for Mr Ainsley to disappear up the stairs before sarcastically singing, "Glassware? Oh, whoopie!" He let out a yell of frustration. It was so sudden that it made Zaiba jump. He turned to the crates of expensive champagne and, one by one, began viciously kicking them.

"Let's see ..." *KICK!* "... how your celebrity ..." *THUMP!* "... likes this!" He gave an extra big kick to one of the boxes then yelped as he stubbed his toe.

Zaiba stared at the crates. If champagne was

anything like lemonade, those bottles would be fizzing with bubbles by now.

Clark gave a final few kicks to the crates. "Clear. *This. Up. Yourself,*" he hissed viciously before storming up the stairs.

Roberto gave out a little whine – Poppy's samosa had finally been eaten up and Ali's distraction technique had lost its charm. It was time to head out.

Swiftly and carefully, Zaiba shuffled over to the door back into the garden, Poppy and Ali following close behind. They crept up the stone steps, blinking at the twinkling fairy lights that laced the path.

"That is *one angry waiter*," Poppy whistled, passing Roberto to Zaiba so she could dust down her top.

"I can't help wondering if Mr Ainsley's attitude has anything to do with the missing dog collar," Zaiba suggested.

"What do you mean?" asked Ali.

"We know that Liza and the waiter definitely don't like him. So how many other members of staff hate him too? And we just heard ourselves that Mr Ainsley is desperate for Maysoon's stay to be a success. So..."

"Oh my goodness!" Poppy breathed. "Sabotage!" She rubbed her hands together. "I love it!"

"We're not here to love it. We're here to solve it." Although Zaiba couldn't resist grinning – if they got this right, they could save the day! "Remember?"

Poppy's hands fell to her sides. "Of course. Detecting is a very serious business." But Zaiba noticed Poppy dig Ali in the ribs and the two of them hide their smiles.

Zaiba looked down at Roberto cuddled up in her arms and felt her own twinge of excitement.

"Come on," she smiled as she stared up at the hotel windows. "I can't *wait* to see the look on Maysoon's face when she sees her little dog again!"

"And we'll finally get to meet her," Poppy reminded her.

The three of them beamed at Roberto who barked in agreement.

Yip!

II
A BITTERSWEET REUNION

It felt like they were walking on air as Zaiba, Poppy and Ali ascended the stairs to Maysoon's room. They beamed as they marched up the gilded staircase. Zaiba almost expected a round of applause from Maysoon's entourage, but she stifled that thought before she got carried away. After all, they still had their biggest investigation to pursue – the case of the missing collar.

Even Roberto could sense he was getting closer to Maysoon as he tugged on the makeshift lead and pointed his nose in the direction of her room. They rounded the staircase and were heading down the corridor when they noticed a solitary figure waiting alone by their hotel room door.

"Uh-oh," Poppy muttered.

"Mariam, what are *you* doing here?" Ali asked as they drew level with her.

Zaiba expected Mariam to frown or smirk or say something sarcastic, but instead she draped an arm round Ali's shoulders and playfully knocked into him. Something wasn't right. It was like Mariam had had a personality transplant.

"What do you mean?" She smiled. "Why wouldn't I want to come and see my favourite cousins? And Poppy..."

Ali wriggled out of her grip.

"Sorry, Mariam, we don't have time to chat," Zaiba said as politely as possible. This was really testing how professional she could remain as a detective. "We have to go to—"

"Find the celebrity?" Mariam finished for her. Her eyes gleamed with excitement.

Oh no, Zaiba thought. *She wants to come with us.* She gripped Roberto's lead tighter. What was she up to?

"I just wondered if ... well..." Mariam shifted about

uneasily. She almost seemed nervous. "I thought I could come with you!"

Poppy actually laughed out loud.

"Absolutely not!" Ali scowled. Zaiba scooped Roberto up and he whined in her arms.

"You think that after you have been nothing but nasty to Zaiba," Poppy began. "After you were mean on her birthday, have been trying to get us in trouble *all day* AND done NOTHING to help us rescue Roberto..." Poppy paused for a breath. "You think after all that, we would let you come with us to meet Maysoon?"

All three of them stared at Mariam, waiting to hear what she'd have to say.

"Um, yes?" Mariam ventured.

"No!" Poppy cried. Red circles had appeared on each of her cheeks. Zaiba began to feel a small pang of sympathy for her cousin, deep inside her. Were those tears brimming in Mariam's eyes? She dashed one away as she realized that the friends weren't going to let her join them.

"Maybe not ... but at least I didn't tell Aunt Jessica

that you were all in the attic!"

Zaiba stepped between Poppy and Mariam. She knew Poppy was just frustrated with Mariam's behaviour, but that didn't mean they had to be mean to her cousin. Just like Eden Lockett's rule number eleven says: *The best agent is cool, calm and oozes charm.*

"Mariam, this is a delicate situation," Zaiba explained patiently. "It's a private reunion between a distraught owner and her loyal companion. Maysoon wouldn't want to meet fans at this time."

Mariam opened her mouth to protest, but suddenly a cold voice called out from the end of the corridor.

"Mariam! What are you doing over there? Did I give you permission to come upstairs?" It was Mariam's mother, standing in an angular grey dress.

"No, Mum," Mariam said quietly. For some reason, she couldn't look at Zaiba and was staring hard at the floor.

"Then come back to the party at once." Her gaze flickered over Zaiba with a look of distaste. "Ah, I see you've found the mutt. You know that celebrity has the entire staff of this hotel searching for that dog?"

Ali quickly placed his hands over Roberto's ears, but it was too late – the pedigree dog gave a small yip at the word "mutt".

Zaiba saw Mariam's mum's thin lips twitch in irritation. "I assume you'll be getting back to your cousin's party straight away, Zaiba. Mariam, come."

Zaiba stood aside to let Mariam pass and her cousin walked quickly down the corridor, keeping close to the wall.

As Mariam and her mum disappeared down the stairs, Zaiba glanced round at the others.

"What was all that about?" Poppy asked. "It's like her mum is a scary headmistress or something."

Zaiba faintly remembered one time long ago when she'd overheard Jessica and her dad talking about Mariam's mum. Something about how uptight she was. "Do you know she has a spreadsheet for when she's planning to throw spontaneous after-school parties?"

Oh my goodness, Zaiba thought now. *What would I be like if my mum was that strict and controlling?* A sinking feeling in Zaiba's tummy confirmed that she might well have turned out as mean as Mariam was. Maybe Mariam wanted someone to hang out with and that's why she was always bugging Zaiba. But then why did she tease them so often? It was certainly a strange way to try to make friends.

Roberto licked Zaiba's cheek, gazing into her eyes. She laughed. "I think someone wants to go home to his mummy." She jiggled him in her arms and Poppy reached to stroke his soft head. "Come on then."

They stepped up to Maysoon's door. A renewed outburst of sobbing from inside the room startled one of the men guarding the door awake. He'd been slumped in a gilt chair and his friend had disappeared. Aunt Fouzia definitely wouldn't approve.

The man blinked up at the little dog in Zaiba's arms. "Is that...?" he began to ask.

"Oh, Roberto," came Maysoon's muffled wails. "How I miss you! What are the latest reports?"

Zaiba heard another voice reply, "Our people have been scouring every room." It was Mr Ainsley. But his people hadn't been scouring the garden, and Zaiba and her people had.

At the sound of his name Roberto gave a soulful howl.

"It's almost as if I can hear your sweet voice now... Hang on!"

Zaiba heard footsteps run to the door.

Roberto gave another *AROOOOOOOOOOOOOOOOOOO* and Maysoon threw open the door.

"ROBERTO!" she sang, her smile breaking out into pure joy. "My sweetie, my angel, my baby!"

"Can I have my belt back now?" Ali pleaded quietly.

Zaiba carefully unlooped the belt from around Roberto's neck and handed him over to his owner. Maysoon spun him round and Roberto gave little *yips* of delight. Zaiba, Poppy and Ali followed her into the room, where Mr Ainsley was glowering at them.

"Shall I call the staff off?" he asked in a low voice.

"Oh yes! Look what these wonderful children did!" Maysoon peppered her little dog with kisses.

Zaiba looked around as Ali gave a low whistle behind her. The room was *certainly* Grand, with a capital G.

There was a huge four-poster bed and a separate room with a red velvet sofa. The carpet was a plush pristine white and the walls were delicately painted with golden leaves. The room was spotlessly clean with any evidence of a busy press interview long tidied away.

Ali made his way over to the flat-screen TV, taking in all its buttons and special features. Poppy caught Zaiba's eye from the other side of the room and mouthed, "Walk-in wardrobe!" with glee. Not to mention a walk-in shoe closet *and* a bathroom with a sunken jacuzzi bath.

Eventually the three of them gathered in the centre of the room to gaze in awe at the star attraction – Maysoon. Zaiba could sense Poppy trembling with excitement beside her and Ali's jaw hung open slackly, even though he didn't like *Swing Sing*. A real-life celebrity in touching distance! Zaiba's hand twitched to take a photo on her phone, but she knew that would be rude. A detective always respected a client's privacy, and at some point Maysoon would notice the missing dog collar. Then Zaiba's investigations would begin in earnest. Her eyes flickered round the room, looking for clues, but the only suspicious thing she saw was the look of fury on Mr Ainsley's face. He should be delighted that his star guest had been reunited with her dog. Why was he so angry all the time? It just didn't make sense. He ran one of the best hotels in town – at the moment the *only* hotel in town taking bookings. Her gaze wandered back to Maysoon.

Maysoon barely noticed the three of them staring at her. She held Roberto up to the ceiling and let his little paws dangle over her. "You are just as beautiful as I remembered. More beautiful!"

"They've only been apart for an hour or so," Ali whispered to Zaiba.

Maysoon finally popped the dog down on a luxurious faux-fur cushion and turned to the friends.

"Thank you so so so so so *sooooooo* much for bringing my Roberto back... Now, tell me who you are!"

Zaiba took charge of the introductions. "My name is Zaiba." She gave her most winning smile. "But I also had a lot of help from my trusted team, Poppy and Ali."

"Team?" Maysoon's eyes shone with curiosity.

The three of them lined up in a row in front of her, beaming proudly.

"We like to solve crimes," Zaiba explained. She noticed Mr Ainsley staring at her. He probably thought they shouldn't be in the celebrity's room, but she wouldn't be put off. She held out her copy of...

"Eden Lockett!" Maysoon took the book from her, turning it over in her hands as though it was a rare artefact. "I read these as a child."

"So did our—" Ali began to explain, but he was interrupted by a fresh howl of displeasure as Maysoon looked at her Italian greyhound, lying against the faux-fur cushion.

"Oh!" Maysoon's face crumpled. "His collar. It's missing!"

"Ah yes, about that..." Poppy started to explain how the collar had been missing when they'd found Roberto in the maze. But her words were drowned out as Maysoon entered another fit of sobbing.

"That collar has a lucky charm attached to it – an even bigger diamond than the ones on his collar," Maysoon explained, pacing the room, her feet sinking into a shaggy sheepskin rug. "My childhood dog used to wear it too and now it's g-g-GONE!"

"A lucky charm?" Ali echoed. "But you know that's—"

Poppy dug him in the ribs to stop him from telling Maysoon that lucky charms were a load of nonsense. At least Mr Ainsley had stopped staring at them – he'd suddenly found an intense interest in the view out of the window.

"Is it worth a lot of money?" Zaiba asked, keeping her voice polite. She assumed that a diamond collar and charm would be worth a lot, and money would be a good reason for someone to steal the collar.

"I need to go and see to the staff." Mr Ainsley suddenly shot across the room. He probably hated Zaiba being so vulgar as to talk about money, but Maysoon barely noticed him disappear.

"Oh yes," the star said as the door shut behind Mr Ainsley. "I have it insured for millions. But that's not the point. I loved it so." She hurled herself theatrically on to the bed, weeping into the deep red linen.

"Oh, don't cry." Poppy patted Maysoon's arm tentatively. "Your fans would hate to see you upset!"

Roberto immediately hopped off his cushion and nuzzled Maysoon, which helped ease the crying a bit. They waited as the star took two short breaths in and then one long breath out with accompanying hand motions.

"My yoga teacher taught me this technique," she explained. "The thing is, I'm here promoting a—"

"*Swing Sing* the movie!" Poppy gushed excitedly.

"How do you know about the film?" Maysoon raised an eyebrow. "I suppose it *is* pretty big news. But this isn't *Swing Sing* ... it's a drama. This film is a big break for me. It's my first chance to be taken seriously as an actor, not just a talent-show judge."

Zaiba nodded and came to sit on the bed next to her and Poppy. Ali was stroking Roberto to comfort him. The dog looked anxious to see how upset Maysoon was. Zaiba was sure that Roberto must feel as emotional as Maysoon—like owner like pet. If they could help Maysoon to feel better, it would probably be good for Roberto too.

"I'm beyond nervous about it," Maysoon continued,

waving a hand dramatically through the air. "We're having this big champagne reception tomorrow where I'll be the centre of attention, but what if everyone hates the film? What if everyone hates me?" She clutched her hands to her chest. "I can't possibly attend without my lucky charm!"

Maysoon threw herself back down and buried her face in the big fluffy pillow.

"But you're *Maysoon*," Poppy said encouragingly. "You're the most talented performer like *ever*. You have nothing to worry about."

At that moment, there was a knock at the door and Maysoon looked up startled. "Could you get that?" she asked Zaiba. "I don't want anyone to see me like this, and my PA has gone out to get me some chocolate."

Zaiba briskly walked to the door, excited that she was *basically* part of Maysoon's entourage now. I mean, if she was letting her answer the doors, what would it be next? Answering the phone? Going to red-carpet events? But Zaiba's stomach sank as she saw who was at the door.

"Damon Harvey, VIPTV. I just wanted to congratulate Maysoon on being reunited with Rodrigo." The journalist was trying to crane his neck round the door, his dramatic black eyebrows arching.

"His name is Roberto and how do you know we found him?" Zaiba pressed, keeping the door closed enough to protect Maysoon's privacy.

"Oh, journalist's intuition," Damon crooned in his corny TV-presenter voice. "Is Maysoon here?"

Zaiba looked back into the room and saw Maysoon shaking her head vigorously.

"No, she's not available at the moment," Zaiba said with a straight face. She'd heard her dad say this on the phone when Jessica didn't want to speak to someone from work. "I think you should leave."

Damon had one last go at peering round the door before he shot Zaiba a flashy smile with dazzling white teeth. "That's a shame. And who are you by the way? Maysoon's secret child? Or maybe she employs children as staff?" Damon's arched eyebrows were wiggling madly at the idea of getting a scoop for his show.

"Stop making things up!" Zaiba was fed up with this guy now. She started to close the door on him.

"Tell Maysoon I'm so looking forward to hearing what she has to say about the new film tomorrow," he managed to add. "I'm sure it will be very *enlightening*."

The door slammed shut and Zaiba stood for a moment, still seething from the rudeness of Damon Harvey.

"See, it's going to be a disaster," Maysoon sobbed. "Everyone knows it! Especially now that I don't have my lucky charm. There's no way I'm going..."

At that moment Georgia came hurrying through the door. "Maysoon, what's wrong?" She stopped in her tracks. "You got Roberto back?" she asked, confused. When the little dog saw her, he buried his face in Maysoon's chest.

"Yes! But look! His diamond collar and the lucky charm are missing!" Maysoon's shoulders sagged and she eased her head round on her neck to roll out the stress. "I think my muscles are going into spasm. Please run me an extremely bubbly bubble bath ...

oh, and call the police!"

Georgia nodded, though her face had turned deathly pale. She faced the friends. "You three should leave. Maysoon needs rest before tomorrow. I've already seen one of those journalists skulking about outside in the corridor."

Before they even had a chance to say goodbye, Georgia had hurried them to the door and practically pushed them out of the room before slamming the door.

"So much for thanking us," Ali grumbled.

"I might never see a walk-in wardrobe ever again," Poppy said. Zaiba could almost see the stars swimming around behind her friend's eyes.

"Come on. We've done everything we can," she told them.

But as they turned back to their own hotel room next door, she wasn't sure she believed her own words. She had a strange feeling in her tummy. They'd found Roberto and delivered him back to Maysoon. That had been the plan all along. But now there was the case of the missing diamond charm. It was as though there were clues whirling all around Zaiba, like the stars in Poppy's eyes. She just had to piece them together and work out what they meant.

12
SNEAKY SIBLINGS

"Psst, Sam. Over here!"

Zaiba, Poppy and Ali were huddled by some trees near to the entrance of the function hall, trying to keep out of sight. Zaiba beckoned Sam over.

"I got your text to meet you, but why are we sneaking around?" Sam looked weary and confused. The night really wasn't working out as she'd planned.

"Well, Sam, you'll be glad to know that we found the dog and he's safely back with his owner." Zaiba took Sam's hand and noticed the henna artist had tried to salvage some of the smeared designs by adding new flowers.

"'Well done, Zaiba. I do feel better knowing there won't be any more canine surprises." Sam's shoulders relaxed a little and she patted Zaiba's cheek.

"But there's more, Sam. An investigation!" Ali jumped up and down, clearly unable to keep in the news any longer. Zaiba slyly nudged Ali in the back.

"It's nothing to worry about though," Poppy quickly added. "Also ... we think we might be able to ask Maysoon to come and meet you."

"Maysoon? Really?" At this Sam's face lit up. "But what's this investigation?"

"I'll tell you more once I've figured it out." Zaiba glanced over her shoulder, to make sure there were no party guests around. Then she turned back to her cousin. "But currently we are on the lookout for a stolen diamond collar!"

Sam nodded slowly and looked at each of them one by one. "Then I think you'd better get investigating. I'll spread the news that the pup's been found."

With a wink and a kiss she walked back into the party, noticeably happier than before.

Poppy and Ali immediately gathered round Zaiba. "Great! So, what's the plan?"

Zaiba took a deep breath. "The investigation is under way. The crime – a missing diamond collar. Now we need to sort through the evidence, examine the suspects and put together some theories."

Poppy and Ali nodded eagerly, hanging on to every word.

"But first..." Zaiba looked over at the door to the function hall. "I think we need to show our faces to Mum and Dad. We don't want them to be suspicious!"

Tuck ... tuck ... swing!

A small crowd cheered as Zaiba's dad swiftly whacked a hockey ball through two sticks marking a makeshift goal. The light had almost gone – but that wouldn't stop Hassan from playing his favourite sport!

"Trust Dad to bring his hockey stick and ball to a Mehndi party," Ali chuckled.

Zaiba sighed but couldn't stop herself from grinning.

As silly as he was, she loved her dad's enthusiasm for hockey, baking – and pretty much everything else!

A small crowd of party guests, including Mariam and her parents, had congregated just outside the patio doors of the function hall to watch Hassan. Aunt Fouzia was even trying to act as goalie until someone told her that wasn't a good idea without the proper body pads *and* a mouth guard. Especially when the shooter could barely see in the fading light!

Now that Roberto was no longer on the loose, it seemed the partygoers had picked up where they'd left off, and several families were giving impromptu song and dance performances.

"Darling, do the trick where you flick the hockey stick round again!" Jessica clapped.

"Don't encourage him..." Ali said under his breath, making Poppy grin. She stole a look at Zaiba to see what they would do next.

After a good ten minutes of cheering on Hassan and a subtle nod at Sam, Zaiba decided it was time to make a move. Jessica had told them to go and help themselves from the dinner buffet. They had to come back to the party by nine o'clock to say goodnight to everyone before going up to bed, but before then they could continue exploring. Thank goodness Jessica didn't realize that "exploring" meant "investigating".

Zaiba gave Poppy and Ali a serious look then jerked her chin towards the function hall. Instantly they picked up on her cue. Checking that Mariam was still fixed on watching the hockey, Zaiba snuck back inside the annexe, with Poppy and Ali following a few moments later.

They emerged into the hall and Zaiba beckoned to them, lifting up the end of the tablecloth. Poppy was eyeing up some skewered chicken that was being brought out to the buffet table but Zaiba caught her hand and dragged her underneath before she could be lured away.

"What's this, our new headquarters?" Poppy grumbled. It was a far cry from the luxury of Maysoon's room.

Once they were all settled beneath the table, Zaiba brought out her detective's notebook and opened up a fresh page. In big capital letters she wrote at the top:

WHO STOLE THE COLLAR?

"Let's think." Zaiba tapped the pen on her chin and thought aloud. "The last time we saw Roberto wearing the collar was in Maysoon's hotel suite while she was being interviewed. So it's most likely to be someone who was in that room."

"What about—" Poppy began, but just as she spoke, Zaiba spotted Mr Ainsley's polished shoes walk past the edge of the tablecloth.

"The hotel manager," Zaiba whispered, once the feet had disappeared out of the room. "Mr Ainsley. He was there, pouring cups of tea, remember? And he's always gliding around so silently ... perhaps he's guilty?"

"Wait a second." Ali shared a confused glance with Poppy. "Mr Ainsley wants his hotel to look posh, not the scene of a crime."

"Yeah, and he's too *sophisticated* to be a thief," Poppy agreed.

But Zaiba had already started compiling a list, ignoring both of them. She made frantic scribbles in her notebook then she held it out for them to read:

EVIDENCE THAT MR AINSLEY IS THE THIEF

- Moves around silently — weird!
- Was at the interview when Roberto was taken off the lead — suspicious!
- Knows the layout of the hotel like the back of his hand. Knew Roberto would have an escape route through our balcony.
- Could get the hotel chef to prepare the meat that lured Roberto out into the maze.

MOTIVES

- Needs the money to restore the hotel.
- Obsessed with lucky charms and glittery objects. This could be a new one for his collection.
- Desperate to get four gold stars.
- Under stress from extra guests/ needs money to deal with the greater demand.

CONCLUSION: GUILTY!

"And I wouldn't be surprised if he was behind those 'accidents' that have been happening around the other hotels in the area." Zaiba raised her eyebrows and crossed her arms.

"Wait just a minute, Zaiba," said Poppy, putting on a stern voice. "Like you always tell me it's innocent *until proven guilty*."

"Yeah, sis," Ali added. "Maybe you just want to solve the case *so badly* you're missing some things..."

Zaiba lowered the notebook and stared at her list, her cheeks flushing. Doubt crept in, making her tummy feel like it was wriggling around. *Am I being too keen? What would Eden Lockett do?*

"OK, are there any other suspects then?" Zaiba looked at Poppy but Ali snatched the pen out of her hand.

"I've got an idea!" Ali quickly began jotting down his ideas.

<u>EVIDENCE THAT DAMON HARVEY IS THE THIEF</u>

- Was also in the room when Roberto's lead was taken off.
- Knew Roberto had been found from the maze before anyone else.
- Snuck up to Maysoon's suite without being stopped - knows how to be sneaky!
- Won't have his reputation ruined by the chaos in the hotel (like Mr Ainsley would).

MOTIVES

- Obsessed with getting a dramatic story about Maysoon to report for his news show.
- Could give him a big break in his career to be able to break the news of the missing pooch.

"You forgot to add 'suspicious eyebrows' in the evidence bit," Poppy said, grabbing the pen. "And I've got my own theories too."

EVIDENCE THAT LIZA THE RECEPTIONIST AND/OR CLARK THE WAITER IS THE THIEF

"Hey," Zaiba interrupted. "Liza was so nice to us, she can't be a suspect. And Clark just got annoyed and kicked some crates. Who could blame him after the way Mr Ainsley spoke to him!"

Poppy tapped the pen against the paper and gave Zaiba a hard look.

"OK," Zaiba said, her shoulders slumping. "Go ahead." All three of them had the right to pursue their investigative instincts, didn't they?

- Also know the layout of the hotel very well. Liza gave the tour in the morning.
- Could easily have got one of the chefs to cook the meat as bait.
- Don't like Mr Ainsley (because he's a total meanie to them)!

MOTIVES
- Get revenge on Mr Ainsley for being so horrible.

- Could quit this job with the money they make from the diamond.
- Feel powerful rather than feeling like Mr Ainsley's puppets.

Zaiba, Poppy and Ali stared hard at the options laid out before them. It seemed like another maze, but this time written down in words.

"Of course it would help if we could get the fingerprints from the dog lead," Zaiba thought aloud. "But then it must have been held by almost every member of Maysoon's staff, including ... what was she called? Georgia! She was quite rude and a little shifty – could she be involved? Although Maysoon seems to really trust her..."

From beyond the buffet table, they heard Mr Ainsley talking to someone.

"Of course, and once again may I apologize wholeheartedly for the uh, disturbance, to your party. I do hope this gift can go some way to make up for it. I wish you all the best with your future wedding and don't forget to leave us a review online."

Zaiba peered from under the tablecloth and saw
Mr Ainsley with Sam and Tanvir. He handed them a
glimmering horseshoe on a satin ribbon. Another lucky
charm. They shook hands and then he quickly glided
off back towards the lobby. SamTan shared a tender hug
before returning to their party guests.

"Let's follow him," Zaiba whispered, clambering out
from under the table once they were gone.

"Zaiba, wait!" Poppy and Ali hurried to catch up with
her.

They slipped out into the lobby and followed at a
distance down the corridor, watching as Mr Ainsley
barked at every single staff member he passed.

"Straighten those tablecloths!"

"Polish those doorknobs!"

"This painting is not perfectly centred!"

With each order his voice became higher until he
was practically singing soprano.

"See," Zaiba whispered. "He's acting suspiciously!"

They arrived in the lobby and hung back by the

sofas as Mr Ainsley approached the reception desk. Some staff members were bringing up crates from the cellar as Georgia took Mr Ainsley aside. Some of the crates had lids in place, but some had already been opened. Zaiba guessed she was going through arrangements for Maysoon's reception the following evening.

"I need all of these crates counted and put in the outside storage, and make sure you dust each bottle. They've been down in the cellar." Mr Ainsley put his hands on his hips and surveyed his staff.

Wait, Zaiba suddenly thought. *Crates from the cellar.* Hadn't those bottles been kicked about?

"Be carefu—" she cried. But it was too late.

A sudden – *BANG!* – came from one of the open crates. Followed by another:

BANG!

Then another:

BANG! BANG!

The champagne bottles were popping after being fizzed up by Clark's tantrum! The movement must have set them off.

POP!

A cork flew past Ali's head and smacked on the wall behind him.

"Aargh!" Ali yelped. Zaiba pulled Ali and Poppy down behind the sofas for cover. Another – *POP!* – sent a cork ricocheting off an ornate doorknob and crashing into an expensive-looking vase, which smashed to the floor.

Then time seemed to slow down as a cork flew towards Georgia...

SMACK!

It hit her square in the forehead. She stood wobbling for a few seconds before her eyes rolled back and she crumpled to the floor.

"Oh my gosh! Ms Stevens, are you all right? Someone send for the doctor, sharp!" Mr Ainsley threw himself down beside her and gently slapped her cheeks, trying to revive her. But she flopped in his arms, like one of Zaiba's old rag dolls.

"Zaiba! Look!" Poppy whispered.

"I know, she's fainted," Zaiba said. "It's OK, Mr Ainsley has it under control."

"No." Poppy gently shook Zaiba's arm. "I mean, look at her designer trainers. They have snakeskin-pattern soles. That's so cool! I think..."

Zaiba sighed. "Not now, Poppy. You can tell me about the fashion stuff later."

"Listen, Zaiba—"

But instead of listening to Poppy, Zaiba was busy watching Mr Ainsley. It was his turn to be led to the chaise longue for a sit down.

"Have you any idea how much that champagne cost? The reception is tomorrow! And now Maysoon's own PA knocked out in my lobby!" He put his head in his hands.

Hmmm. That funny feeling returned to Zaiba's belly.

"Would he really ruin his reputation for a diamond collar?" she mused.

"*Now* you're getting us." Ali nudged her.

"But if Mr Ainsley doesn't have the diamond collar, could it be Liza or Clark? Or even Georgia? I mean, Clark is clearly angry with Mr Ainsley, and he was also mean to Liza. And no one is closer to Maysoon than Georgia..."

The three friends stared at each other as she left the thought hanging in the air.

Georgia Stevens, Maysoon's PA, was lying stretched out on the sofa in the lobby, an ice pack pressed against her head. The hotel medic had checked her over and deemed her perfectly fine (apart from the large red bump forming on her forehead). To prevent a further media storm, Liza had placed an ornate screen in front of her to give her some privacy as she recovered. The rest of the staff carried on with their duties as usual, helping other hotel guests with their evening plans. Zaiba noticed a few of the Mehndi party guests had torn themselves away from the buffet to come and see the drama that was taking place in the lobby. Word spread fast in this hotel!

Zaiba, Poppy and Ali were free to stare from their hiding spot behind the sofas as, moments later, a familiar face entered the lobby with a dustpan and brush to sweep up the broken vase.

"Clark," Zaiba whispered, watching intently as the waiter bent down next to Georgia and began sweeping.

"He's like a bad pimple, he just keeps popping up," Poppy said, screwing up her nose.

He moved across the floor, closer and closer to Georgia, whose head turned to one side, and then suddenly he was behind the screen. From this angle, the pair were only visible to the three young detectives. As Clark ducked further behind the screen, their heads came close and Zaiba saw Georgia's lips moving rapidly.

"Are they whispering to each other?" Poppy said, her eyes bulging.

"Seems like it," Zaiba replied.

"Look at his shoes, they're covered in dust," Ali said, frantically tapping Zaiba's shoulder.

Mr Ainsley never allowed any dust inside the hotel and it had been a while since Clark had been in the cellar... So where had he been recently? "Ali, your detective instincts—"

"I know, they're really coming on." Her little brother rolled his eyes. "You should have more faith in me!"

But Zaiba was already peering harder at the soles of Clark's feet as he and Georgia continued to whisper.

"Look," she said. "The prints on his soles... Where have I seen those before?"

"His soles have zigzag prints and Georgia's shoes have snakeskin. *That's* what I was trying to tell you earlier!" Poppy hissed. "We saw them on the hidden staircase."

Zaiba looked at Poppy. "I'm sorry, Pops. I should have listened to you."

Poppy gave her a reassuring smile. "Oh, it's fine! We've got them now!"

"But got them doing what?" Ali asked confused.

That was the one question Zaiba couldn't answer—yet.

13
THE LAST PIECE OF THE PUZZLE

Zaiba's mind started going into overdrive as she pulled her crime-solving partners further back behind the sofas. From there, they crawled towards a better hiding place behind the plant pots, keeping their bodies folded low. If they were going to go over their theories, they needed to make sure they weren't going to be disturbed.

"Right," Zaiba said, as they crouched down. "The footprints we saw on the hidden staircase were snakeskin and zigzag prints! But why were Clark and Georgia in the secret staircase? Perhaps they were casing the joint before they put their plan into action? This Clark guy, he's been everywhere. The Mehndi party, Maysoon's suite, the cellar...

Remember that conversation with Mr Ainsley? The hotel manager was horrible to him. Maybe he wants revenge!"

Zaiba pulled out *Eden Lockett's Detective Handbook*. She flicked through the pages until she came to her notes from that afternoon. "There —" she pointed to the page — "in the cellar, Mr Ainsley called Clark 'Mr Stevens', and do you remember what Georgia's last name is?"

"Stevens!" Poppy said, wide-eyed.

"So they could be brother and sister?" Ali said.

"Those sneaky Stevens!" Poppy scowled.

Zaiba shut her eyes and thought hard. There was something else, something important...

"Ah!" She clicked her fingers and her eyes snapped back open. "Aunt Fouzia said that they tried to book another hotel but the manager called her up to cancel. The manager's name was Mr Stevens!"

"Which hotel was that again?" Ali was struggling to keep up.

"The White Hall," Zaiba said.

Poppy screwed up her face as she remembered. "*WH*, the letters on Georgia's pen!"

"And it was Georgia who handed that chef a fifty-pound note earlier... It could have been for the plate of bait."

Zaiba quickly scribbled down their findings in her notebook:

- Georgia + Clark = siblings
- White Hall Hotel manager Mr Stevens — their dad?
- Footprints on the hidden staircase, same as their shoes — why were they sneaking around?
- Clark sabotaging the champagne in the cellar.
- Georgia bribing the chef to make food that would lure Roberto out into the maze.
- Mr Ainsley horrible to Clark — revenge?

Zaiba paused. The footprints *were* on the hidden staircase, before Mariam came and scuffed them away! But they weren't there now. Oh no! All the air in her chest deflated.

"We can't prove that Georgia and Clark were on the hidden staircase," she said. "There's no proof of their footprints any more."

Ali suddenly scrabbled around in his pockets and starting tapping on his phone.

"Um ... hello, Ali? We're in the middle of a crime-solving conundrum right now!" Poppy said.

"Aha! I knew I took a picture." Ali turned his phone round triumphantly to show a high-definition picture of the footprints in the dust on the hidden staircase. "See, with the time stamp and everything."

Zaiba and Poppy gave each other a look before launching themselves on to Ali in a massive hug.

"You genius! That could be crucial evidence," Zaiba said, squishing her little brother even tighter.

"OK, OK, now get off me," Ali wheezed.

Zaiba let him go and placed her notebook back in her bag.

"Are we going to tell everyone?" Ali asked excitedly.

Zaiba shook her head. "Not yet. There are still too

many parts of this puzzle we don't understand. Why would they have stolen the diamond collar? Where *is* the diamond collar? Why were they on the hidden staircase? And how did they even get in there? No one had used the lobby entrance to the secret staircase for ages — remember all those cobwebs!"

Ali's grin spread across his face.

"What?" Zaiba grabbed his arms. "Tell us!"

He unpeeled himself from her grip. "Well, remember when we were in Maysoon's room, and you two were fawning over the sunken jacuzzi?"

"Yes?" Sometimes little brothers could be really irritating. "So what? You were looking at the flat-screen TV!"

Ali shook his head. "I wasn't just looking at that. I was looking at the locked door too."

"What locked door?" Poppy asked. "Was it part of the walk-in wardrobe?"

"No." He took a deep breath, explaining as though Zaiba and Poppy were tiny children. "Zaiba, give me your map of the hotel."

She grappled in her little yellow bag and pulled it out. Ali pointed to the rooms on the west wing of the hotel. There were a few rooms that ran next to the hidden staircase under the turret in the central lobby. He tapped a finger against the side wall of the biggest room that was right next to one of the landings on the hidden staircase. It was Maysoon's room.

"Oh my!" Zaiba breathed. "That's the door out on to the secret staircase. One of the locked doors we passed on the way up. Someone could have used that door to get on to the staircase."

"Exactly." Ali passed back the map to her.

"We're so close to solving this investigation," Zaiba said. "I can just feel it!"

Peering out from behind the plant pot, Zaiba saw that the lobby area had emptied. Even Georgia and the screen had gone. *Phew, they sure worked fast at this hotel!*

"Come on, you two – it's all clear," she told the others. They emerged from behind the plant pot and noticed a large banner being wheeled in for tomorrow's champagne reception. The staff were already getting the private lounge ready. A large picture of Maysoon in black and white was adorned with giant lettering that read "Introducing Maysoon in her first breakout role!"

They had no idea that Maysoon had decided she couldn't face going to the reception. Zaiba imagined the star up in her room now, packing her bags ready to leave before the most important event of her career had even begun.

Then she thought of her parents enjoying the Mehndi party and checked her watch. It was getting late and they'd told Jessica they'd come back to the party by nine o'clock. If they didn't solve this crime soon, they never would. Zaiba's parents would come looking for her, Poppy and Ali to take them up to bed!

Checking to make sure the coast was clear, Zaiba pressed firmly on the spot at the top of the wooden panel that hid the secret staircase. It popped open! She stepped into the gloomy passage with the others following, lighting the way with her phone torch. The panel door slid shut behind them.

Back in their secret place again, Zaiba felt a thrill of excitement. Ali wasn't so keen. "I hope those spiders have gone to bed," he said, his voice trembling despite the joke.

"You've done so well at facing your fears, Ali! You've come back in," Zaiba pointed out.

"Oh yeah... I guess I am getting braver," said Ali, his chest puffed out. He walked a little faster.

They trooped up the steps. When they reached the second floor, Zaiba once again tried to open the door, rattling the handle.

"Still locked," she confirmed.

"Maybe it used to be a servant's door," Ali said. "This building goes back to the eighteenth century, you know."

Does he know everything? Zaiba wondered.

Poppy pressed her ear to the door and closed her eyes. Zaiba could see her detective's mind whirring and felt a flush of pride. But as she watched Poppy, Zaiba heard something too – the woeful sound of someone singing. After a few moments, Poppy began humming to herself.

"Oh no, Poppy's gone mad up here in the dark!" Ali threw his hands up to his face in pretend dramatics.

But Zaiba could see her friend was on to something. "No, listen!" She put her finger to her lips and she and Ali listened to the faint words floating through the door. Soon Poppy was humming louder and louder, then she was singing along, until she leaped round.

"It's Maysoon's number one single, *Dance, dance, dancing the night awayyyy!*" Poppy sang. "This is Maysoon's room. The door in there that Ali couldn't open – this must be it! Check out the floor," Poppy added with more confidence. "Look! You can still see the zigzag footprints."

They bent down and studied the footprints. It was hard to tell from all the scuffmarks, but they could just make out that the zigzag footprints were heading downstairs.

"Those are Clark's prints, perhaps from when he was heading down to the cellar to sabotage the champagne?" Zaiba said.

"Look!" Poppy said. "A new set of snakeskin footprints – those are Georgia's. And they're heading upstairs!"

This time Zaiba took the lead, racing up the last flight of stairs to the little attic room. They burst through the door into the room with its rows of old iron beds.

"Why would Georgia come up here?" Zaiba asked.

Zaiba began pacing the room, her mind going into overdrive. She tried to remember every single golden rule in Eden Lockett's books to give her some kind of clue. *Had Georgia come up here to hide?* No, she had nothing to hide from, and besides, she was downstairs, recovering in the lobby. *Maybe this was a shortcut to somewhere?* But that didn't make any sense either.

As Zaiba thought, Poppy's eyes widened. "Oh my goodness," she began to murmur. "Diamonds!"

Ali and Zaiba exchanged a look. "Excuse me?" Zaiba asked.

At that moment, music floated up from the party downstairs. Poppy folded her arms. "What has this whole investigation been about?"

"Er, a VIP, a runaway dog and some funny footprints?" Ali suggested.

"No!" Zaiba snapped her fingers. "The actual crime –

the missing diamonds!"

Poppy grinned. They were totally on the same page.

"Right... But why would the Stevens siblings take them, and what's that got to do with this dusty old attic?" Ali asked, a frown creasing his brow.

"Why are we here today, at the hotel?" Poppy prompted.

"Because Mum likes to torture me by forcing me to wear suits?" Ali replied.

"Because of family! We love Sam and wanted to be at her Mehndi party – we'd do anything for her. Right?" Zaiba asked.

"So that's what Clark and Georgia are doing," Poppy explained. "They'd do anything to help each other. Perhaps they wanted to save their parents' hotel? What with the malfunctioning self-check-in machines and having to turn away a VIP they must be in trouble..." Her face had turned red. "And where better to hide the diamonds than a dusty old attic that no one knows exists?"

Zaiba's mind went into overdrive. "Hidden treasure..."

Ali caught up with their thinking and feverishly

looked around the attic room.

"Poppy, did anyone tell you you're a genius!" Zaiba cried.

But her friend was one step ahead of her, already opening and closing drawers.

"People stash their treasures away to come back for when it's safe. Go through everything. Ali, help!" Zaiba ordered. "Quickly! Georgia didn't come up here to hide, she came up here to hide *the collar* until it was safe to sneak out of the hotel. After everyone had gone, probably."

Poppy and Ali began scurrying around the room, running from servant's table to dresser, dragging open the stiff wooden drawers and sending up clouds of dust until—

"There!" Zaiba called out. She'd spotted the tiny glimmer of something. She ran to the drawer and pulled it all the way open. There, in the corner, something glittery poked out from under some paper.

"Roberto's collar! And the lucky charm!" Poppy clapped her hands together and jumped up and down.

Even in the dim light of the attic room, the diamond moon and star shone and sparkled.

"We should be careful. Unlike the lead, there won't be many fingerprints on the collar. We don't want to smudge the criminal's prints."

Ali whipped a silk napkin out of his pocket that he'd been carrying snacks in. He carefully picked up the collar with the napkin before giving it to Zaiba. "Shall we hand it over to the police?"

Zaiba shook her head. "Not quite yet. After all, *I've* done the detective work."

Ali cleared his throat loudly.

"I mean, *we*'ve done the detective work." She threw her brother and best friend a grateful glance. "We should be the ones who confront the criminals, don't you think?"

This would be the last piece of detective work, slotting everything into place. If she managed to get the brother and sister to admit to their crime, it would be case closed. Her first real case – it was like a dream come true.

Zaiba took Poppy and Ali's hands and squeezed them. "We've done it. We've cracked the case. Now let's get those Sneaky Stevens to confess!"

14
GOTCHA!

Bursting out of the hidden staircase panel and into the bright lights of the lobby, Zaiba heard a familiar voice.

"Zaiba, Ali, Poppy! What on earth have you been doing?" Jessica demanded, standing with her hands on her hips. She and Hassan no longer appeared in a party mood – both of their expressions were like thunder! She glanced at Zaiba's outfit. Zaiba didn't even want to think about how dirty and scruffy they looked this time.

Another figure appeared. Aunt Fouzia placed a comforting hand on Zaiba's shoulder and squeezed. "I think Zaiba has discovered something interesting. Sam tells me you've been doing some investigating."

"Investigating?" Hassan looked ready to explode. "That's not why you're here. We promised Sam this would be the best party ever!"

"But Dad, we've solved the crime!" Zaiba cried out.

"What crime?" Jessica's expression darkened. "Mariam told me that Zaiba might have something to do with the missing diamond collar, but I thought she was just telling tales."

Zaiba clenched her teeth. *Mariam. Just when I was starting to understand that girl...* Then Jessica spotted the diamond collar and charm, wrapped in the napkin in Zaiba's hands and her eyes widened.

"It's not what you think," Zaiba said quickly. "Mariam only knows half the story!"

"Then I would like to know the full story," a voice purred from behind the reception desk. Mr Ainsley had appeared silently from his office and was now looking intently at the collar in Zaiba's hands.

Aunt Fouzia stepped forwards with an evidence bag, into which Zaiba dropped the collar. "Mr Ainsley, I need you to call an emergency meeting. Zaiba has something

to tell everyone. This is official business." She flipped
open a sleek leather card case to reveal her official
government ID.

Agent Fouzia Sharif
Official Affiliate of the Pakistani
Republic Government
SNOW LEOPARD DETECTIVE AGENCY

In that moment, Zaiba loved her auntie more than
ever before. Aunt Fouzia had everyone in the room under
her command in a split second — she was a true top
agent!

"Certainly, Agent Sharif," Mr Ainsley responded.
"Personally, I shall be very grateful indeed to have these
mysterious goings-on solved once and for all. I will
prepare the lounge."

"And I'd like to know what my children have been
up to when they were supposedly 'innocently' exploring
the hotel!" their dad said. The three of them kept
their heads bowed, not wanting to meet Hassan and

Jessica's stern gaze.

As Mr Ainsley went to give some instructions to a group of waiters, Zaiba noticed a figure by the main entrance where guests' luggage was already piled up. The figure bent to a leather suitcase and began to heave it out of the front door, moving quickly – too quickly. A corner of the suitcase bashed against the door and the waiter quietly swore to himself, kicking a foot into the doormat. Just like the person who'd kicked the champagne crates. It was Clark, trying to get away!

"Aunt Fouzia," she whispered, fear crawling over her.

"Don't worry, I've seen." She raised her voice. "Stop him!"

Mr Ainsley whirled round and nodded at the doorman, who immediately snatched Clark's collar and dragged him back into the hotel, delivering him to the hotel manager.

"Well done, Mr Rollings," Mr Ainsley remarked. "What would we do without you?"

The doorman blushed with pride. That must have been the first nice thing Mr Ainsley had ever said to him.

"Now, everyone to the lounge," Aunt Fouzia commanded, dialling a number on the reception phone. "I'm going to ring up to Maysoon and ask her to join us. She needs to hear this."

"How do you know the phone number to her room?" Poppy asked.

Aunt Fouzia simply tapped her nose. Was there anything she didn't know?

Everyone had gathered. The only sound that could be heard in the lounge was the ticking of the clock as a room full of people sat waiting for the truth to be revealed. Mr Ainsley and Liza were standing by the doors, in case someone tried to make a run for it. Zaiba, Ali and Poppy perched on velvet stools while Jessica and Hassan sank down on to a sofa, never once taking their eyes off the children. Sam and Tanvir had also come to listen, hoping to get some answers for the destruction of their Mehndi party. They looked just as glamorous as before, Tanvir was still in his sharp grey suit and Sam had changed into an emerald-green lengha, but their eyes were red and their faces crumpled. It had been a long day. By the time everyone had gathered it was already ten o'clock, way past their agreed bedtime!

Zaiba felt eyes burning into the back of her head and turned round. Mariam was standing at the door, watching.

"If you've come to gloat, Mariam, I'm sorry to disappoint you," Zaiba said.

Mariam furrowed her brow. "Actually I—"

"Zaiba isn't in trouble." Ali stuck his tongue out. "No thanks to you!"

A hand rested on Mariam's shoulder. It was her mum. "Come on, Mariam, time to go," she said, leading her away.

"But I wanted to see—" Mariam protested.

"I said, time to go!" From the look on her mum's face, she wasn't messing about.

Mariam sighed, looking sad. Zaiba realized that Mariam hadn't said a word to them as they'd thrown their taunts at her. Maybe she hadn't been here to make more trouble. Maybe she just wanted to see the conclusion to Zaiba's investigation? She watched Mariam being led away by her mother and wondered when she'd see Mariam again – and if she was ready to be friends yet.

Jessica leaned over and placed a hand on Zaiba's knee, speaking in a low voice. "Her mum can't help it," she said. "Her own mother was very strict, you know."

Jessica was so good at guessing what Zaiba was thinking – she was the best stepmum in the world, even if she did get a bit agitated about a few cobwebs and streaks of dirt.

Zaiba smiled at her.

"I'm lucky to have you," she said, and Jessica squeezed her knee. Without thinking, Zaiba stroked her little yellow bag where *Eden Lockett's Detective Handbook* was stored, as though to reassure her ammi that she'd not forgotten her. Because she never would. Having two mums could be complicated sometimes, especially when one of them wasn't there.

"What's all this?" Zaiba's thoughts were interrupted by Maysoon appearing in the room. She wore a big fluffy bathrobe and had pink ostrich-feather slippers on her tiny feet. She carried Roberto, cradling the Italian greyhound in her arms. His tail wagged wildly when he saw Zaiba and he gave a little yip of greeting. "I was in the middle of my bubble bath!"

Georgia was following close behind her, still busily answering emails on her phone. But as soon as she caught sight of Clark being held firmly by Mr Rollings, she dropped her phone and made a dash for the door.

"Not so fast, Ms Stevens, we'd like to have a word with you." Mr Ainsley smiled, smoothly stepping forwards to block her way.

Roberto barked another little excited yelp.

"I know, I know, sweetie," Maysoon soothed him. She looked around the room with a pained expression. "Someone, please tell me what the emergency is?"

Zaiba held out the diamond collar, with the diamond charm dangling from it.

"You angel! You've found my lucky charm!" Maysoon cried, taking the bag. She started to hand Roberto to Georgia but Zaiba quickly called out, "I wouldn't do that if I were you."

Maysoon clutched Roberto closer to her chest and shot Georgia a confused glance. "Why? What's going on?"

Georgia gave her boss a shaky smile and went to stand at the edge of the room, pressing herself against a wall. Mr Ainsley shut the door with a click, before joining Liza in front of it. There was no escaping now. Not for anyone.

Zaiba caught Aunt Fouzia's eye and saw her encouraging smile. Now was the moment that Zaiba had been waiting her whole life for – the big reveal.

Her stomach churned a little and her hands shook. She'd never spoken in front of this many adults before. But then she remembered her ammi's note in *Eden Lockett's Detective Handbook*. She closed her eyes.

Better put on my brave pants today!

Standing up in front of the captive audience, she first turned to Clark and Georgia. "Would you mind coming to the front of the room and showing everyone the bottom of your shoes?" she said in a loud clear voice.

"And why am I taking instructions from a child?" Clark scoffed.

"That child is more mature than you'll ever be. Now do as she says," Aunt Fouzia ordered. "Or would you rather we have the police *take* your shoes off for you?"

The siblings looked annoyed but lifted their feet reluctantly, revealing the snakeskin and zigzag prints.

"Great. Now, Ali, please show the room the photo you took on the hidden staircase." Clark stiffened, a look of horror crossing his face as he realized why he'd been made to show his shoes.

"A hidden staircase! In my hotel?" Mr Ainsley seemed alarmed.

Ali ceremoniously held out his phone and walked around the guests in a slow semicircle, his nose proudly in the air.

As the phone passed Sam, she spoke up. "These footprints are the same as the soles of their shoes."

"So what if we used a staircase?" Clark snarled.

"Yes, what exactly are you accusing us of?" Georgia remarked, folding her arms.

Zaiba heard her father whisper to Jessica. "It's just

like an episode of *Murder, Most Red*."

She took a deep breath. "Georgia and Clark, I have reason to believe that *you* stole Roberto's diamond collar."

There was a shocked gasp from the room and Zaiba felt the hair on her arms stand up at the thrill.

"The hidden staircase leads to an attic. An attic where we found the collar and the lucky charm. Also ... we believe Clark and Georgia are siblings."

There was a screech from Maysoon. "Georgia! You told me you were an only child, just like me." She hid her face in Roberto's fur.

"This is ridiculous." Clark pouted. "I won't listen to this from a *little girl*."

"If I might jump in," came Liza's timid voice. "Perhaps we should wait for the police to get here to begin their investigations."

Aunt Fouzia spoke in such a crystal-clear way that the whole room froze. "Zaiba, Poppy and Ali have done all the investigating. *They* will lead the proceedings. Now please, no one interrupt Zaiba again."

Liza nodded. Zaiba was slightly disappointed that the receptionist didn't have faith in her, but her auntie definitely did.

Mr Ainsley moved to the centre of the room and stood before the grand fireplace, smoothing down his jacket. "Why were you down in the cellar earlier, Clark, when I *specifically* asked you to polish the glassware?"

"I-I was checking the champagne, remember?" Clark stammered, cracking slightly under Mr Ainsley's gaze.

"Ah yes, the champagne that popped all over the lobby this afternoon?" Zaiba said, piling on the pressure.

Small beads of sweat were forming on Clark's brow. Georgia kept her gaze fixed firmly on her brother. Zaiba didn't think she'd blinked once in the last thirty seconds!

"Now, Clark," Zaiba continued. "Please tell everyone where Mr Ainsley hired you from last minute?"

"The White Hall Hotel," Clark mumbled.

"We nearly had our Mehndi party there!" Tanvir said.

Zaiba nodded, walking over to Georgia, and then slipped the pen from her shirt pocket. "And where

Maysoon was meant to have her press party. Until the self-check-in machine *mysteriously* went haywire and everything was cancelled. It's also where Georgia got this pen that she's been using since she arrived here. It's their father's hotel!" Georgia tried to snatch the pen back but Zaiba popped it in another evidence bag she'd been given by Aunt Fouzia.

Clark dabbed at his forehead with one of his long sleeves.

"The self-check-in machine mixed up everyone's names – they lost all the booking details," Georgia blurted out.

"So it was just a coincidence then." Zaiba raised her voice slightly. "That you both ended up *here* right when two big events were planned."

Mr Ainsley narrowed his eyes and took a deep breath. "You're Graham Stevens' children..." he said in a grave voice. "He and I have known each other since napkin-folding training. It brings me no joy that I will have to tell him his children have been committing crimes in my hotel!"

"You know their dad?" Zaiba asked.

"Why of course," Mr Ainsley replied. "All the hotel managers in this town know each other. Once a year we meet to exchange tips." He turned to Clark. "I taught your father everything he knows about folding napkin swans, so I will give you two options. Either you confess immediately or I ring the White Hall and tell your father myself!"

There was silence. Clark and Georgia looked at each other and Zaiba swore she saw Clark's bottom lip tremble. Clearly their father was not a man to mess with!

Zaiba knew this was the time to strike. "Clark and Georgia, I am accusing you of not only sabotaging the other hotels in town, but also taking off Roberto's lead, luring him into the maze using the smell of prime steak—"

"Wait, WHAT?" Maysoon said in horror before Aunt Fouzia shushed her.

"And finally stealing his diamond collar to stash away in the attic, ready to take later. My only question is ... *why did you do it?*"

This was it. The moment Zaiba had been waiting her whole life for. Would Georgia and Clark confess, or would her reputation be ruined before she'd even started her journey to becoming the best detective of all time?

15
CRIMINAL CONFESSIONS

"Please, Mr Ainsley, don't tell Dad!" Clark cried out, his face crumpling into panic. "He already thinks I'm good for nothing. I was going to use the money to start my *own* hotel, so I could show him I'm not useless after all!"

Georgia finally blinked and rushed over to her brother's side.

"I thought if I could get rid of competition from the other hotels before mine even opened, I'd be sure of success," Clark continued.

Georgia patted her brother's shoulder and sniffed back tears.

"So you sabotaged your own father's hotel to

get ahead?" Hassan interjected.

Zaiba slowly reached her hand into her purse and pressed "record" on her phone. She wanted to get Clark's confession on tape, clear and simple.

"Yes, OK!" Clark snapped at Hassan. "And I knew I couldn't steal the diamond if the event happened at the White Hall. Not with Dad breathing down my neck the whole time. So I broke the self-check-in machine ... those things are stupid anyway!"

Mr Ainsley smirked a little.

"You stole Roberto's diamond collar to get money?" Zaiba prompted.

"Yes," Clark snarled, his head in his hands. "When Georgia got the job as Maysoon's PA I saw the opportunity. She paid off the chef to hide the steak out in the maze, slipped off his lead and then I was there to take Roberto's collar when the mutt showed up."

"He isn't a mutt," Maysoon sniffed. "Georgia, I can't believe I trusted you."

A few silent tears fell from Georgia's eyes. She couldn't even bring herself to look at Maysoon.

"But how did you know that we'd leave the door open for Roberto?" Zaiba asked.

Clark laughed nastily. "You just made our job quicker and easier for us!"

Zaiba felt a slight flush of guilt but pressed on. None of this was her fault. "And why didn't you run away once you had the collar?"

Clark suddenly stopped laughing and fixed her with a stony glare. "What, you can't work that one out for yourself, great detective? If I had run away I'd immediately have been a suspect. I was planning to set up a new hotel here in town – I couldn't be a wanted criminal!"

Zaiba felt her brain ticking over as she joined up the dots. "You got Georgia to hide the collar up in the attic, using the servant's door in Maysoon's suite. And you snuck down to the cellar using the secret staircase."

"I was so close to getting away with that diamond," Clark spat. "And I wanted to leave a nice parting present for *him*." Clark jutted his chin at Mr Ainsley.

"You mean ruining thousands of pounds worth of champagne and covering my vintage cheese in dust!"

Mr Ainsley was outraged.

"Sneaky Stevens," Poppy tutted.

"But how did you know that the staircase existed?" Zaiba wanted to be sure she had every detail of this case locked down.

Clark's eyes darted about until finally Georgia spoke up. "Actually, that was me," she said in a small voice. "I used to read these books when I was little and the author writes about a hidden staircase at this hotel. I never wanted to be a criminal – I always wanted to be a detective!"

Zaiba and Poppy stared at each other in amazement, their mouths wide open. *Georgia was an Eden Lockett fan?* Zaiba couldn't help feeling a little more sympathetic towards her. It really seemed that Clark had forced her to be part of his plans. Zaiba loved her brother too, but she would never let him steer her towards a life of crime!

The sound of approaching police sirens cut through Zaiba's thoughts. Everyone in the room began shifting around, preparing for the upcoming drama.

"Before the police arrive, I would like to say that I feel

betrayed by you, Georgia," Maysoon declared, standing up from the gold seat where she had been perched. "However, I don't think you're entirely at fault. Clark is clearly a bad influence on you. But to put an innocent animal in danger is unforgivable." She gave Roberto a little kiss and clasped the collar, still in its evidence bag, tighter. "Roberto and I *trusted* you." She shook her head and slowly sat down just as three police officers arrived at the door to the lounge.

"Good evening, officers," Mr Ainsley greeted them and he and Aunt Fouzia began speaking with them confidentially.

Zaiba watched as the three police officers listened intently to Aunt Fouzia before looking up at Clark and Georgia. They gave a small nod before two of them walked over to the siblings, reaching for handcuffs in their back pockets.

"No ... please, I'm sorry!" Georgia cried. But she held out her hands limply as they were handcuffed. Clark on the other hand did not say a single word. Instead, he stared at Zaiba with his small icy-blue eyes.

Zaiba returned his gaze, taking a deep breath and drawing herself up tall. Thankfully the third police officer approached Zaiba, and Clark looked away.

"I hear we have you to thank for some stellar detective work," she said, bending to shake Zaiba's hand.

"No problem at all," Zaiba said in her best adult voice. "There's also a dodgy chef in the kitchen I think you should go and question. Oh, and I have some evidence to submit. I've alphabetized it here on this sheet of paper, including the crime scenes you should go and dust first."

LIST OF EVIDENCE IN THE CASE OF THE MISSING DIAMONDS

- Diamond dog collar and diamond charm (dust for prints)
- Dog lead
- Phone recordings taken in hidden staircase and cellar and of confession
- Photo of the plate of meat that lured Roberto to the maze (CHECK THIS CRIME SCENE AND DUST PLATE FOR PRINTS)

- Photos of Clark and Georgia's footprints in the dust
- White Hall Hotel pen

The police officer smiled. "You're very thorough. I'll have my boss go and question that chef. Now I must speak to the victim. I can't believe I get to meet Maysoon..." She winked and gave one last handshake to Ali and Poppy.

More police had arrived now and they were questioning other staff members. Among the hubbub, Zaiba just managed to see the sneaky Stevens as they were led out to the police car. Zaiba felt a pang of sadness in her stomach. She was glad that the crime had been solved, but she knew what it was like to want to impress your parents. Had the siblings just been silly and naïve?

"You did the right thing." Aunt Fouzia approached, giving Zaiba a hug. "And solved your first crime! It's hard to watch, but criminals must see justice done."

Zaiba's dad ran over and scooped Zaiba up in a hug. "My superstar! Listen, I'm sorry I was hard on you. But it's for a good reason. When your ammi went missing ... it made me worry about you even more."

"It's all right, Dad. I understand." Zaiba smiled and hugged her dad tightly. She knew he worried, but that just meant he loved her!

Jessica sidled up beside them. "Zaiba, honey, I'm sorry I was so strict about your clothes. If you'd just told me what you were doing..."

"We couldn't," Zaiba explained, patting her bag with *Eden Lockett's Detective Handbook* in it. She recited from memory, "*Revealing your findings before the crime has been solved can hinder the investigation!*" She paused. "And I couldn't have done it without Ali and Poppy."

"We'll win awards for being the best detective's assistants ever!" Poppy cried, linking her arm through Zaiba's.

There were murmurs of appreciation from everyone in the room as they looked over at Zaiba, Poppy and Ali. They'd really solved a crime. A real-life crime!

"What an evening!" Maysoon sighed dramatically, bringing the attention back to her. "It's already eleven o'clock! Now Roberto and I really must get our beauty sleep before tomorrow's reception."

"You mean, you still want us to host it here?" Mr Ainsley brightened.

"Why, of course." Maysoon smiled. "I have my lucky charm back." She ruffled Roberto's fur and the little charm, freshly dusted for prints, tinkled on his glittering collar. "As long as you think you'll be able to get enough champagne."

Mr Ainsley immediately began ordering staff all over the hotel to resume preparations. "Reorder the champagne, ready the cheeses, pay double if you have to!" He paused and then added, "Please."

He shot out of the room. The Royal Star was back in business and maybe its manager was going to be a little less strict from now on.

Maysoon started after him, but then she turned to Zaiba and her family.

"You should go to your rooms and get some rest too. After all, being VIP guests at a champagne reception can be very tiring work." She winked and flounced out,

Roberto following her with an excited *yip*.

"Did she just invite us?" Sam's jaw almost dropped to the floor and she embraced Tanvir, hopping up and down in excitement. "We're VIP guests at a celebrity champagne reception! How many couples get *that* as a present on their Mehndi night?"

Zaiba grinned. She and her friends hadn't just saved Sam's Mehndi party – they were going to help Maysoon celebrate in style too!

16
BEST DAY EVER

"This is the BEST day of my life!" Poppy squealed as she tried on her fourth outfit of the evening. This one was a floral silk dress with matching print leggings – it was a masterpiece. They were getting ready for the champagne reception and Maysoon had arranged for a local boutique to bring outfits for the girls to try on.

In addition to being invited to Maysoon's party, Mr Ainsley had arranged for Zaiba, Ali, Poppy, their parents, Aunt Fouzia *and* the engaged couple to stay in the hotel for an extra night after the reception, "Free of charge of course!" Although there hadn't been much rest going on last night as Zaiba and Poppy had been far too excited to sleep.

"I'm going to go and show Maysoon this outfit," Poppy said, rushing out of their room. She was fully taking advantage of being friends with a famous celebrity.

Zaiba smiled and went to rummage in her suitcase for a pair of tights. She had opted for a deep purple gown. It was the only dress she'd ever worn that reached all the way down to the floor. As she searched, her hand touched something hard and she moved aside the socks and PJs to uncover another of her Eden Lockett novels. It was book number six, *The Hidden Staircase*. The book that was inspired by this very hotel. She must have packed it by accident. Picking it up she flicked through the pages, stopping to have a look at each of the little notes her ammi had written across the margins. One stood out in particular. *The most exciting mysteries are the ones left unsolved!*

Zaiba wished she could solve the mystery of what happened to her ammi, but where would she even begin? A tear crept down her cheek and she quickly wiped it away.

"Sweetie, is everything all right?" It was her dad, coming to check whether she was ready to leave. Hassan came over to the bed and sat down next to Zaiba, his arm resting on her shoulder.

"Dad, did Ammi ever leave anything else for me?" Zaiba asked, her voice a little wobbly.

Hassan sighed and picked up the book. He gently placed it back in the suitcase and then took Zaiba's hands.

"Zaiba, you know I usually say leave the past in the past. I've been waiting to tell you something and, well, I can see that you're old enough now and your love for detecting isn't just a phase..."

Zaiba held her breath and looked up into her dad's eyes. They glinted as if he was remembering something ... remembering *someone*.

"Your ammi," Hassan began, "started the Snow Leopard Detective Agency with Aunt Fouzia."

Zaiba's mouth flew open.

"She was an agent too. It was on one of her missions that she went missing and passed away, which is why I can get so worried about you investigating. I'm sorry, Zaiba."

Zaiba paused before throwing her arms round her dad. "Sorry? Why? This is great! My ammi was a detective just like me!"

Hassan looked at Zaiba with quizzical eyes before he chuckled and squeezed her back, even tighter.

Zaiba smiled and breathed in the scent of him.

In a fit of giggles Poppy rushed back into the room, twirling her floaty silk dress round in a circle.

"Maysoon says this is the one!" She beamed.

"Then I guess it's time to go down," Zaiba said, her face brightening.

Hassan went to get Jessica and Ali. Jessica had even given Zaiba one of her best handbags to put her Eden Lockett book in for the evening. And Ali... Ali was wearing his favourite hoody!

Opening the door, Zaiba saw Hassan, Jessica and Ali waiting in the corridor, matching smiles on their faces. They were going to arrive all together, as a family. Just as it should be.

Sitting among the stars, glitz and glamour, Zaiba felt like she was dreaming. The private lounge of the Royal Star Hotel had been transformed overnight into an A-list venue. The chandeliers were sparkling, all 314 crystals in each, and there were candles lit in every corner of the room with important-looking people gliding about in expensive gowns and suits. Liza had been allowed to attend and she and Mr Ainsley were busy greeting guests. It looked as though they'd put their disagreements behind them. It was like a scene in a film and, for once, Poppy was lost for words. Ali was freely running across the polished floors and then sliding on his knees to the music. Zaiba shook her head. They couldn't take him anywhere!

"Esteemed guests," Mr Ainsley announced from a small podium in the centre of the room. "Please join me in welcoming the star of the evening, Maysoon."

Everyone clapped and Maysoon appeared in the doorway in a beautiful turquoise cocktail dress. She smiled confidently with her head held high. Even Roberto seemed to have a confident air, with a matching bow on his collar next to the lucky charm.

Once the fuss around her had died down, Tanvir approached Maysoon respectfully. "Maysoon, would you mind taking a picture with my fiancé? She's such a big fan of yours and it would make our uh, extended, Mehndi party so special."

"Why, of course," Maysoon sang in a cheerful voice. "Let's take a selfie!"

Sam gleefully rushed over to Maysoon's side and the two women took quite a few pictures together, chatting away happily. Finally, Zaiba heard Maysoon say, "I can't wait for the wedding!" Sam's favourite celebrity was going to come to her wedding! Zaiba felt her tummy flip over.

Next it was Zaiba, Poppy and Ali's turn for pictures. Tanvir was photographer, making sure to include the beautiful surroundings of the room.

"I'm going to upload this one straight away and write just how wonderful my stay here has been," Maysoon said, smiling at Mr Ainsley. Zaiba looked over Maysoon's shoulder and watched her add four golden star emojis

to the caption. Mr Ainsley was sure to get those four stars now!

"This is the best night of my life," Mr Ainsley said in a small voice.

"Hey, same here!" Poppy laughed, giving him a high five. He didn't quite know how to do it, but Ali showed him.

"Like this!" He held up his hand and slapped Poppy's then Mr Ainsley did the same. Zaiba bit her lip to stop herself from laughing, while Mr Ainsley ran a hand over his head as though that was the most rebellious thing he'd ever done. It probably was.

Zaiba went to sit on a plump-cushioned chair and take in the scene. Sam and Tanvir were giggling together and watching Aunt Fouzia dance with Hassan and Jessica. Zaiba felt a huge smile stretch across her face. She'd managed to make SamTan's Mehndi party unforgettable *and* made her parents proud. She might not have her ammi here to see her success, but she had her notes and her Eden Lockett books. Not to mention her partners-in-crime-solving, who were rushing over to her.

"Maysoon is going to take questions from the press now," Poppy said excitedly, sitting down next to Zaiba. "You'll be happy to know that Damon Harvey was ejected from the building for trespassing!"

"Good riddance!" Zaiba waved her hand in the air.

Ali glanced around the packed room. "Did you know that roughly two thirds of journalists are men?" he said, sharing another of his facts.

Poppy raised her eyebrows, thinking. "If being a detective doesn't work out, maybe I can be a journalist!"

Before Zaiba could say what a great idea that was, a reporter from Channel One Entertainment began the questions. "What inspired you to take this career move, Maysoon?" he asked.

"Well, there's a little dog here with an expensive taste for organic dog treats and diamond collars," she joked easily. Then she turned more serious. "Also, I wanted to push myself. To see what I am capable of doing, which turns out is a lot!"

The journalists laughed approvingly and Maysoon caught Zaiba's eye across the room. She blew her a little kiss and Zaiba felt deep down that Maysoon was sending her the same message. *You can be anything you want to be!*

The questions went on and Aunt Fouzia came to join the three detectives-in-training at the back of the room. She leaned down and hugged Zaiba. Aunt Fouzia was dressed like a secret agent in a Bond film, in a floor-length black gown with diamond earrings.

"You've made me so very proud this weekend. Your eye for detail really shone through. You know, perhaps..." She cocked her head on one side, thinking, and Zaiba held her breath. Then she clapped her hands together. "Perhaps it's time to open the first unofficial UK branch of the Snow Leopard Detective Agency."

Zaiba and Poppy's eyes grew wide. "Really?" they said in unison.

"Could I have a break first?" Ali groaned. "I'm not ready for any more spiders or small dark spaces."

They giggled and Aunt Fouzia looked at Maysoon, speaking so easily in front of the crowd of people.

"If Maysoon can achieve her greatest ambitions, then why not you?" she said to Zaiba.

Sam came over to join her mum and looked down at her cousin. She was going to make the most beautiful bride ever. "I have every faith in you, Zaiba. You rescued my happiness this weekend and I can't thank you enough."

Zaiba felt so proud of herself. She'd gone from hiding beneath a table to solving the biggest crime to ever hit the Royal Star Hotel. All because her aunt had encouraged her. And, of course, her brother and her best friend had helped. They'd achieved so much together! Though she still wasn't sure she should ever share the secret of climbing down the hotel trellis.

"Tut, tut, Samirah," Aunt Fouzia corrected her, smiling down at her niece. "This isn't just Zaiba any more." The room stilled, and it was almost as though everyone was waiting to hear what she would say next. "This is Agent Zaiba now."

Her family cheered and Zaiba glanced around, taking in the smiling faces. She'd done it, she'd actually done it! She'd become a detective, just like her aunt, and she hoped that – somewhere – her ammi felt proud. Zaiba felt as though she was floating on a cloud. But more than that, she felt a tingle of excitement pass over her. Poppy and Ali appeared either side of her and scooped her up in a hug. Then they pulled back and gazed into each other's faces, their eyes shining bright.

"You know, guys," Zaiba whispered. "This is just the beginning."

"Totally!" Ali said.

Poppy gazed down at her dress. "You know, I'm going to have to invest in a whole new wardrobe. What *do* detectives wear?"

Zaiba laughed and dug her hand into her new handbag, pulling out her Eden Lockett book. She stroked a hand down the cover of *Eden Lockett's Detective Handbook*. Maybe one day, books would be written about Agent Zaiba! She bit her lip, smiling to herself. Well, if she wanted that to happen, she'd just have to start solving more crimes...

DO YOU HAVE WHAT IT TAKES
TO JOIN ZAIBA AND THE SNOW
LEOPARD DETECTIVE AGENCY?

TURN THE PAGE
TO FIND OUT!

THE HIDDEN STAIRCASE
BY EDEN LOCKETT

EXCLUSIVE EXTRACT

My heart thumped, keeping time with my knuckles as they rapped against the wooden wall panelling.

Tap, tap, tap, thunk.

My knuckles stopped; my heart galloped faster. That part was hollow! I knew it!

The house was centuries old, just the kind of place where long-forgotten secrets lurked in nooks, crannies, chimneys and walls.

There must be a secret passage behind here. All the windows and doors had been locked when Lady Thornside's diamond tiara had disappeared. No one had left the manor house since, which could only mean—

"Eden Lockett, why are you leaning against my walls?" came an imperious voice from behind me.

I wheeled around to find Lady Thornside peering at me, a mixture of curiosity and anger in her face.

You can't shush a lady. But I put my finger to my lips, hoping she'd get the hint that this was a time to be quiet.

"Lady Thornside, I am investigating," I whispered. "It's very important that you leave me to it."

She arched an eyebrow and nodded, whisking past me into her magnificent drawing room. I waited until the butler closed the ornate doors behind her.

Thank heavens. I turned back to my work. "If there's a secret passage, there must be a secret way to get into it," I muttered to myself. I prodded the panelling, searching for a button or a handle or something.

Nothing.

That's when my knee brushed something on the wall — a very slight raised knot in the wood. I watched, my hand over my mouth, as the panelling creakily slid open.

There, behind the wall, was a hidden staircase.

A shadowy, musty staircase, with footprints leading from step to step, up into the darkness.

Taking a deep breath, I stepped inside.

Can you spot one key difference between how Eden opens the secret to door to her staircase and Zaiba finds her own secret set of steps?

EDEN LOCKETT'S TOP DETECTIVE TIPS

🔍 Blend into the background and observe. Listen, watch and smell your surroundings for vital clues.

🔍 Draw a map! Mark entrance and exit points – you never know when a high-speed chase might occur...

🔍 Make notes. Suspects, evidence and motives all need to be recorded.

🔍 Keep your fellow detectives safe and keep their spirits high! Snacks are good for this purpose.

🔍 The Golden Rule – Keep calm and carry on detecting!

DETECTIVES IN TRAINING!

Being the world's best detective takes lots of practise!

SEE HOW GOOD YOUR MEMORY IS...

Practise your observation skills with your friends.
Collect about twenty objects – the more random the
better! – and give your friends thirty seconds to look at
them. Once the time is up, cover the objects. Each person
has two minutes to write down as many of the objects as
they can remember.

How did they do? Now it's someone else's turn to choose
the objects!

MAKE YOUR OWN FINGERPRINTING KIT!

To make a fingerprinting kit you will need:
- clear tape
- flour
- a paintbrush
- white paper
- a pencil

Practise taking fingerprints by finding a flat surface
(with fingerprints on!). Brush the flour on to the surface
so it covers the fingerprints then gently blow off any
extra flour. Stick some clear tape over the flour and
you'll have collected a potentially useful clue!

You can also take fingerprints from potential suspects!
On a piece of paper, colour in a patch with a pencil.
Ask your suspect to rub their finger hard on the pencil
marking then place their finger on to the sticky side of
some clear tape. Gently lift their finger off the tape and
stick the tape to a plain piece of paper. Compare it to any
fingerprints you found at the scene of the crime!

SECRET CODES

If you're working on a top-secret investigation, you'll need to use code to communicate with your fellow detectives. Here are some ideas to get you started:

1. **Reverse words** – by reversing the letters and the order of the words, you can confuse anyone trying to intercept your message! Can you work out what this says?

STNIRPTOOF EHT WOLLOF

2. **PigPen** – each letter corresponds to the part of the grid it is found in. What does this message tell us to do?

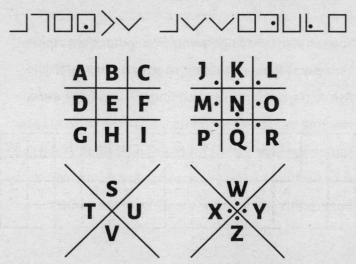

3. Morse code is an established form of communication using dots and dashes. It is especially useful as you can write it, or use sounds or light to make it!

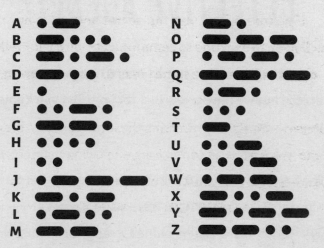

INVENT YOUR OWN CODE!

Use a grid like the one below to create symbols to represent different numbers, letters and punctuation. Make sure your symbols and drawings are simple and easy to reproduce so everyone in your team can use it.

A	B	C	D	E	F	G	H	I	J	K	L	M
N	O	P	Q	R	S	T	U	V	W	X	Y	Z

JOIN THE SNOW LEOPARD DETECTIVE AGENCY!

Aunt Fouzia swears that an agent never shares her secrets, but we have a few just for you! Did you know...

The first Snow Leopard Detective Agency was set up in Karachi, Pakistan, by Aunt Fouzia and Zaiba's ammi in 1999. For years the sisters helped a range of clients. Now Aunt Fouzia is the lone head detective.

Aunt Fouzia has become a legend for cracking all sorts of cases, including crimes that involved a prime minister, a famous Bollywood actress and even the Karachi Stock Exchange!

Snow leopards are rare big cats which can be spotted (if you're lucky) roaming the mountains of Pakistan.

Snow leopards are feisty, great at camouflaging themselves and love exploring even the harshest of environments – just like the very best detectives!

Aunt Fouzia's brain works best when she drinks lots of tea. Her record is ten cups of chai in one day!

Now the new unofficial UK branch of the Snow Leopard Detective Agency is up and running, with their first case solved! Will Zaiba, Poppy and Ali let any other agents into their top-secret organisation?

DETECTIVE FACT FILE

Now you know what it takes, fill in your detective fact file to join The Snow Leopard Detective Agency!

Your name: _____

Key skills: _____
_____
_____
_____
_____

Fears: _____
_____
_____
_____
_____

Favourite famous detective: _____

_____

Favourite fact: _____

_____

_____

_____

_____

Favourite investigative accessory: _____

_____

_____

_____

_____

MEHNDI MADNESS QUIZ!

Can you sort fact from fiction with these Mehndi party questions?

1. Mehndi parties only happen in Pakistan.

False! Mehndi parties originated in South Asia. But as people have migrated across the globe, you can find people celebrating them all over the world. You might also hear a Mehndi party called a henna party. In Pakistan it is called the Rasm-e-heena.

2. The Mehndi party takes place before the wedding.

True! Pakistani weddings are made up of several ceremonies. The Mehndi party usually takes place a few days before the wedding ceremony which is called the Shaadi.

3. Only women are allowed at a Mehndi party.

False! Traditionally, Mehndi celebrations were held for women but nowadays everyone gets together to celebrate!

4. Henna is a type of food.

False! Henna is the coloured paste applied to the bride and groom's skin in intricate designs. Henna is the English word for Mehndi.

5. Henna paste is a reddish-brown colour.

True! Henna is made from the leaves of a henna plant, crushed up and formed into a paste. When it dries it turns a dark brown colour on the skin.

ABOUT THE AUTHOR

Annabelle Sami is a writer and performer.
She grew up next to the sea on the south coast of the
UK and moved to London, where she now lives, for
university. At Queen Mary University she had an amazing
time studying English Literature and Drama, finally
graduating with an MA in English Literature.

When she isn't writing she enjoys playing saxophone
in a band with her friends, performing live art
and swimming in the sea!

ABOUT THE ILLUSTRATOR

Originally from Romania, Daniela now lives and works in Cambridge and is completing a master's degree in children's book illustrations at the Cambridge School of Art.

Her passion has always been children's illustration and she loves to draw kids, cats, plants, girls in cool outfits and cute little objects! Creating a magical mix of the ordinary and extraordinary Daniela loves to highlight subtle detail and find beauty in everyday life.

HELP ZAIBA SOLVE HER
NEXT CRIME IN...

Agent Zaiba
INVESTIGATES

THE POISON PLOT